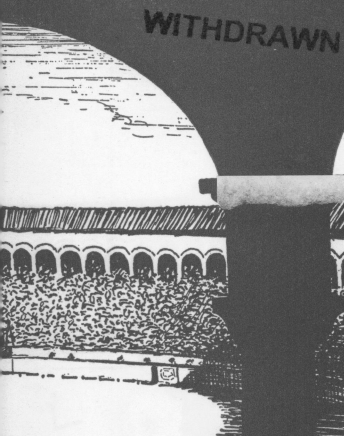

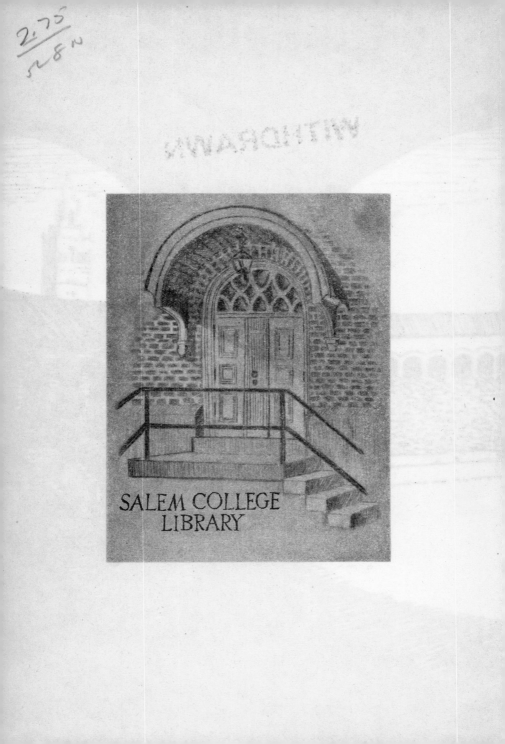

Matador

by Barnaby Conrad

ILLUSTRATED BY THE AUTHOR

ADOR

HOUGHTON MIFFLIN COMPANY BOSTON
THE RIVERSIDE PRESS CAMBRIDGE

BOOKS BY
BARNABY CONRAD

The Innocent Villa
Matador

FIRST PRINTING. DECEMBER, 1951
SECOND PRINTING. MAY, 1952
THIRD PRINTING JUNE, 1952
FOURTH PRINTING. JULY, 1952
FIFTH PRINTING, JULY, 1952

The Riverside Press
CAMBRIDGE · MASSACHUSETTS
PRINTED IN THE U.S.A.

The deep bass chords began
at five in the afternoon.
The bells of arsenic and the smoke
at five in the afternoon.
On the street corners groups of silence
at five in the afternoon.
And only the bull with heart uplifted!
at five in the afternoon.

"Lament for Ignacio Sánchez Mejías"
— FEDERICO GARCÍA LORCA

Author's Note

THE READER is asked to remember that the Art of Tauromachy is centuries old, that only the outcome, not the ceremony, varies, that the banderilleros are usually older men, the picadors usually fat, the bulls usually black, and — according to Blasco Ibáñez — the only beast in the Plaza de Toros is the crowd.

Therefore, any tale of bullfighting must follow the same essential pattern. Though the events described in this book are as true to life as the author can make them, the characters themselves, with the exception of the great matador Juan Belmonte who makes a brief appearance, are entirely fictitious.

Matador

IT WAS a very special day, this Sunday in May — not only for Sevilla, the spiritual capital of bullfighting, but for all of the Iberian peninsula and even for many countries in Latin America. People had come from all over Spain and Portugal and many parts of Europe, and what tickets there were left to be scalped by the "revendedores" were going for as high as one hundred and fifty dollars.

It was a very special day because Francisco Torres y Nuñez, called Pacote, the greatest matador of his generation and considered one of the three greatest bullfighters who ever lived, had been goaded into a last performance after having announced his retirement. For killing two Miura bulls he would receive the unequaled sum of thirty thousand dollars, six times the amount of the average matador. But that was not the reason he was fighting, for in his eight years as a senior matador he had made four million dollars, and he had no desire for more money.

He had come from his big home in Córdoba with his entourage the day before the fight and was installed in a

1

suite at the lavish Hotel Andalucía Palace. The hotel is three hundred yards from the sluggish, tree-lined Guadalquivir River and only a few blocks away, hugging the river, is the ancient plaza de toros, La Maestranza. Hours before the fight, people who could not afford a ticket had waited along the boulevard and lingered at the sidewalk cafés to watch him make this last trip to a bull ring, the beginning of the end to an amazing career.

At three-fifteen, the first fancy carriages began to clop down the Paseo de las Delicias. Some of the women in them wore mantillas and Manila shawls and the men broad-brimmed glossy Cordobés hats.

By three-thirty the street was jammed with archaic taxis, big foreign cars belonging to falangistas, carriages belonging to royalty, and people — hundreds of people streaming to fill the fifteen thousand seats of the Maestranza.

At three-forty-five the big blue station wagon pulled out of the courtyard of the Hotel Andalucía Palace, the canvas cape basket strapped on its top.

It forced its way down the swarming boulevard slowly but relentlessly, actually pushing people aside with its front fenders as it did its best to deliver its owner to the place he least wanted to go in the world.

An old woman in rags spotted the gaudily uniformed man sitting slumped in the back seat next to his manager, and rapping on the window of the car she called fervently: "God protect you, boy, God protect you!"

He stared back at her with unseeing eyes as the car moved on and his fingers unconsciously went to the scar that notched the left side of his chin. At twenty-nine, his face was sad and drawn and old, yet at the same time it was compelling and majestic. If he were to walk into any café in any part of the world people would immediately ask: Who is this young-old man — for he had the look and aura of Number One. Hod carrier, dancer, artist, banker, one might not know — only that he was the best in his field.

The hundreds of other Sevillanos didn't have to wait to see the familiar profile. Who else in Spain had such a car? Besides its external splendor, it was built especially for a bed to be made in the back so that the matador could snatch some sleep while traveling across the country between fights; in his best years he had fought every other day for the entire six months season, sometimes twice on the same day in different towns, and there was little time for rest. At the sight of its blue magnificence wedging through the humanity, men standing at the bar in the bodegas along the river said, "Here he comes," and hurried to gulp down their cafés con leche or pay up for their anís; the bullfight is the only thing in Spain which begins on time.

One little man in a beret and dungarees put down his "chata" of beer and stood up on his toes to look over the crowd in front. "Vaya, vaya!" he murmured. "What a car! How would you like to have a coach like that?"

His companion, a little drunk, clapped him on the shoulder. "And how would you like to have got it the way he did, eh, old one?"

"Did you see his face? He looked different."

"How would you look if you were going where he's going?"

"No, he looked strange. I talked to him only a few

hours ago. I talked to him at noon, and he didn't look like that. You don't believe me? It was before you arrived. Ask the barman. I talked to Pacote and he talked to me, just like anybody, just like you or me. We had a cognac together and a crayfish. But he didn't look like that. Ask the barman if you don't believe I talked to him. Oye, barman, come over here and . . ."

"We better get going," the other said. "Or we'll find someone in our seats."

The big station wagon had already turned off the boulevard at the corner by the monumental stone coliseum that was the Maestranza, and it fought its way through the bulging narrow street that led to the back of the arena. Unlike most plazas de toros, the back of the Maestranza melts into clusters of houses and bodegas that over the centuries have mushroomed in the damp shade under the stands, around the patio de caballos, and up against the base of the structure. People were hanging out of windows and flowered balconies around the little cobbled square, and they cheered when the car pulled up in front of the entrance. The driver sprang out and hurried around to open the rear door. The thin broad-shouldered man in the glistening gold and white "suit-of-lights" emerged slowly, almost painfully, and the shouts became louder.

"Olé tu madre!" called a man from the balcony of one of the houses built up against the plaza. This would be all he'd see of the show, for the cheapest ticket would have cost him the equivalent of his family's food for a month. But he would hear the tormenting sounds from the arena excitement all afternoon and he would imagine what was happening and curse his poverty. But now he made the most of this one moment. He brandished his hand in front of him for emphasis and shouted, "Olé Don Paco, olé gran maestro!"

The gaunt figure stood by the car uncertainly for a few moments, his melancholy eyes blinking at the people massed around him, his face greenish-white under the black, knobbed hat. The little bald, fat man bustled out of the car, and he and another bullfighter elbowed through the crowd to convoy the matador up to the big gate. He winced under the masculine pats on his back and shoulders, and when a woman tried to kiss his hand he jerked it away. The small door cut out in the big gate creaked open and the men stepped in. The matador tripped on the sill, but the fat man caught him, and the door was slammed.

Inside the courtyard were the photographers, ten of them, and the men from the No-Do, the official newsreel, who started grinding their old-fashioned camera.

"There's nothing to photograph yet," the little fat man growled. "Save your film."

The photographers snapped pictures as the matador walked toward the gate that led to the patio de caballos. But then, as they passed the latrine, a roofless, doorless cement structure, the matador hesitated, turned, and went in. A photographer started to follow, but the little fat man batted the camera out of his hands and blocked the doorway.

"Can't you even leave the man alone for this?" he said, his bald head as red with anger as his face. "A man can't even go here without photographs?"

The photographer retrieved his camera from the ground, looked to see that the lens wasn't broken, and said abusedly: "Caray, Pepe, you know me — Santana from the A.B.C. I wasn't going in there to take any pictures."

Another photographer in back said out of the corner of his mouth: "The gentle, bald Pepe is acting very strange today."

"Not as strange as Pacote," said the man next to him. "I don't know what's wrong, but something is. I hope I've got enough film. I think we're going to need it today."

Pacote Torres stood before the trough inside the latrine. He was swaying slightly.

"Jesús, Jesús," he mumbled. The nostrils of his aquiline nose flared as his water revived the stench of thousands of urinations before him.

What a day. Good Christ, what a day this had been. And what a day it was going to be. It hadn't started so bad. It hadn't started so much worse than any of the others.

1

THE FIRST SOUND he heard that day — the day that
was to be the most terrible and most glorious of his life —
was a shotgun going off. It woke him up with its *pumff*.
Then a pause and *pumff* again.

Probably missed it, Pacote thought sleepily, with that
long pause between shots. He wished he had nothing more
on his mind today than going out to the tiro de pichón.
Not that he liked killing the pigeons. As a matter of fact
he hated it. The Duke of Pinohermoso had taken him out
once and insisted that he try it. Pacote was a rotten shot,
having tried it only a few times before in his life, but he
couldn't miss after yelling "Pájaro" and the box trap was
sprung and the bird didn't even have time to get its wings
open before pellets ripped it into a puff of feathers. He'd
put down the gun and didn't shoot again, and they'd all
laughed at "the great killer, the fearless Pacote."

But still, killing pigeons would be nice today — instead.
Anything would be nice, instead. A ride around the hills
in back of his ranch in Córdoba would be the pleasantest

7

of all. He was a rotten rider, too, but it would be good. Especially with someone who didn't ask him questions about bulls. Socorro maybe. It would be nice with her.

He let himself doze on this for a while, but in his state of half awakeness he got stuck like a cracked record on one scene: he couldn't make the bit stay in the horse's mouth. He would get it in, fix the chin strap, and then just as he was about to get on the horse, he would find himself putting the bit in the horse's mouth again. It went on and on and was so frustrating and exhausting that he made himself wake up. He flung the covers from him. Then he slowly propped his skinny frame up and sat on the edge of the ornate brass bed, his face in his hands. Now that he was fully awake he knew his hands would be trembling when he took them from his face.

Yes, it was really there inside him, as big as an ostrich egg. The fear organ was right there just below the V of his rib cage, below his heart, a great hunk of fear. It was as real as any other organ in his torso. It wasn't the dull ache of the usual fear: this was a sharp pain of fear, unlike any other he'd ever known.

Well, I've a right to it, he told himself. A great big right.

He reached out and absently patted the little gray dog sleeping at the end of his bed. It raised its head to acknowledge the salutation and then dropped the mustached muzzle on its forepaws again. It had a pair of surprised and plaintive black eyebrows that always made it look as though it had just backed into a hot radiator, and it smelled of old age.

"Aí, Compadre, how you stink," said Pacote affectionately.

To show he'd heard, the dog gave a token wag of its tail, like a slowed-down metronome, but he didn't open his eyes.

Pacote looked at his watch, the watch his mother had given him the day of la alternativa, the watch that had engraved on the back: "My son, do not worry, do not be afraid." It was past eleven. Slept ten hours and still exhausted. They'll be here soon. It would be better, in a way, when they got here. It was always bad in the morning because that was when you were you. Later it was better because you became somebody else and something else.

Then for a moment he had a great idea, an idea that made him warm inside and dulled the fear pain: get dressed in a hurry, take the Buick out of the garage, drive to Cádiz, and hop the Marqués de Comillas bound for South

America. It was nice to think about for a few minutes — a little farm in Peru and a beautiful Peruvian girl whose face was blurred but vaguely like Socorro's, only fine and decent. Then he gave a grunting mirthless laugh at himself to make him come back to today, now, this minute, reality.

It's true, he said. You are through, you're finished, your nerves are shot. You need a drink. He looked across the big hotel suite at the bottle on the dresser. He'd almost killed it last night, but there was a little left. It made him sick to think of it with the hangover fuzz in his mouth, but it would feel good once it was down. God bless los Yanquis. They could make whiskey. To hell with Spanish wines.

He started to go for it. Then he said: You fool. You've really turned into a cowardly fool. Drink on the day of a fight — a fight like this one? That's what Niño de Ronda used to do and look where it got him. You're just fool enough to drink on the day of your last fight and get a nice high colonic from a horn. If you were fool enough to get into this thing, you ought to have brains enough to do it right.

He snapped the switch of the little radio on the bedside table. "This is Radio Andorra," said a reedy female voice "presenting for your — " He twisted the dial and the B.B.C. from Gibraltar had time to say: "In the two years which the Labor Government has — " before he sped on to another station and the martial strains of "La Morena de Mi Copla." The music faded and a voice boomed, "Toros in Sevilla! Today everyone is — " He snapped the radio off.

The door opened and a white-faced middle-aged man came in. It was Matagatos, his cousin and peón de confianza — his number one banderillero. He was carrying a lot of cheap paper fans and a photo and a dozen telegrams and cables.

"Buenos días, Pacorro," he said, forcing heartiness. He jerked the shade and let it tug halfway up. The Andaluz sun was blinding.

"Hola," Pacote grunted, shading his dark eyes. "Hola, Catkiller. Has Chaves picked up a third banderillero?"

"I don't know. I haven't seen him yet this morning. I just got up."

"A ver," he said taking the telegrams. "Let's see." They were blue and not in envelopes but just folded and pasted. He ripped through them, not reading their platitudes but just glancing at the signature, looking for hers. There was none from her, and he threw them aside.

Matagatos handed him the fans, a pen, and a telephone book to write on. Pacote opened the first fan. A slip of paper clipped to it said: "Please dedicate to Juanita Pérez, a great admirer."

There were some pictures printed on the fan of Pacote in action, and on each side was his sad-faced portrait under which was written simply "The Best." It was a tragic face, a strong face, an ascetic face, a face El Greco would have enjoyed painting. The prominent nose was aquiline, and the heavy-lidded eyes gave an aristocratic mien. It was a scarred face that might easily emerge as ugly in a photograph, and when analyzed in a mirror it distressed the owner. But it was not ugly. It was a fine face.

He wrote on the fan in his careful, elaborate hand, the

hand of one to whom writing was an unaccustomed task: "To my friend Señorita Juanita Pérez, excellent aficionada, from her servant, Francisco Torres y Nuñez "Pacote.""

Now what the devil would she do with his precious signature? Ordinarily he hated this business, but now it was diverting; it took his mind off: *Today, today, today!*

"Here's another," said Matagatos.

To an unknown person named Luis Morales he wrote on the photo, forming the words with his lips as he wrote: "To my good friend and companion . . . "

Maybe Morales ran a bar here in Sevilla, and he would hang up the picture there and tell his customers he was an intimate friend of The Number One. Maybe the picture would be worth money, if he were killed today. "Last photo ever signed by him," the man would boast happily as he . . .

If he were killed today!

He shoved the fans away. "I'll finish these later," he said in his deep Cordovan accent. He folded his hands tightly together so that Matagatos would not see them tremble.

He could hear heavy breathing out in the hall and then the door of the suite opened and his manager waddled in. José "Pepe" Chaves was little and fat with big dark glasses and a black toupée that was always askew and generally cocked over one eye; it was treated more as a beret than a wig, and sometimes it went into his breast pocket as a kind of hairy handkerchief. He had the Sunday newspapers under one arm and he dumped them on the bed and sank into a chair.

"Going to be a scorcher today," he puffed. His rough face had an unfinished look about it, as though it had been made by a series of angry punches at a chunk of red putty. But there was a gentleness in the face, a sort of rough gentleness. "Hotter than the sea." As to all Andaluces, the sea to Pepe was a variable commodity used to make any statement more emphatic. "Hola, Matagatos." He slid the toupee off his head and fanned himself. "See what your friends in the newspapers say, Paco? I hope they develop sores on their feet and be made to carry the mail."

Pacote dragged over a paper to him and began to read it, his hand propping up his chin. The front page had a picture of him and one of Tano side by side. He was a smooth, smug twenty-year-old. How ugly my picture is next to that young bastard, Pacote thought. He began to read aloud:

"Sevilla and people from all over Spain will witness one of the most exciting duels since the Joselito-Belmonte rivalry thirty years ago," it said underneath Julio Salazar's by-line, "when the great Pacote — called the Monstrous One because of his prowess and ability to charge fantastic prices! — "

"Sweet little termites, aren't they?" Chaves grunted.

. . . "fights what he claims is his last fight with the sensational newcomer Tano Ruiz. Upon returning from his highly successful Mexican and South American campaigns last month, Pacote, aged twenty-nine, announced that he was cutting the pigtail and retiring to his Córdoba estate to raise bulls for others to fight. However, since he has not fought on Spanish soil for some ten months, he has decided to have the last corrida of his life in his beloved Andalucía, those sonsofbitches" . . . he kept reading as though this interjection were part of the text . . . "it is also said that his decision was prompted by the fact that he wished to prove to fans of young Ruiz once and for all that the Old Maestro is still Number One by giving him a lesson in the art of tauromaquia that people will never forget. Everyone knows of the now famous incident between them at a certain Madrid restaurant, and that there is no gran amor between them, and . . .

"Mierda!" Pacote exclaimed, shoving the paper away and standing up. "What are they trying to do to me? I told them I was not going to do anything today — told them I was going to coast! They said they'd take it easy on me. They can't expect me to commit suicide on the last one. I wouldn't have taken the fight if I didn't think everyone knew it was just a farewell exhibition."

"They didn't have to build up all this hay about the rivalry." Chaves flung his toupee on the floor disgustedly. "The paper at the box office is all sold anyway. People want to see your last fight, just to say they saw it."

"And that beloved Andalucía stuff," said Pacote. "I let myself get talked into this one because of the pesetas, and that's all."

Neither one wanted to mention the newspaper's reference to the café incident, the real reason he was fighting today.

"Hui, that dog stinks," said Chaves.

"So do you," said Pacote.

"You should have him put away."

"We should have you put away."

Chaves took out a cigar. "I think I can get Cantimplas for a third this afternoon."

There was a timid knock on the loor. "Adelante," snapped Pacote. "Come in."

A bald, shabbily dressed little man came. "Buenos días, señores," he said.

It was Cayetano Montoya, "Niño de Ronda," once called "the perfect matador."

What in Christ's name does he want, Pacote thought. That's me in fifteen years, if I weren't getting out. Bald as a chamberpot, bags under the eyes like wineskins, eyes as bleary as poached eggs from liquor and maybe dope, and the once beautiful build now sagged into round-shoulderedness and a pot belly. He remembered the book by the American where Cayetano — only the author called him Pedro Romero — went off with the English lady. Wavy-haired Cayetano was nineteen, top man in all Spain, and as the writer had said — "the best-looking boy I have ever seen." Well, he must have had just a few too many English ladies, or something; at forty-five he looked sixty.

"Matador," Cayetano began humbly, looking at the floor and rubbing one hand over his shiny head. There was not even any fringe at the base — it looked as though there'd never been any hair on that head at all, and that he had eyebrows seemed surprising. "I hear you are short a banlerillero today. I happen not to be engaged today, and I was wondering . . ."

The classic prototype of the old bullfighter. Christ's sake, did he have to come around today of all days to illustrate what a lousy business this was? Everyone knew he "happened not to be engaged" for a long time. He hadn't fought as a matador for fifteen years, except in small-town festivals. He had put the sticks in a few times for his son who was a second-rate novillero, but the son's manager had thought it too big a risk to have a drinking banderillero, so his son fired him.

Pacote shook his head. "You heard wrong, man. We're all squared away for today."

They did need another peón, and he would have liked to have helped el pobre, but it was too dangerous. All right to have somebody like Cayetano around when you were fighting calves at a festival, but if someone made a mistake with these bulls there'd be blood spattered all over the sand.

"I really need — I mean, I think if I had one fight in a good cuadrilla I might sort of, you know, get back on my feet." He frowned earnestly, trying to give more conviction to his mumbled words. "I'm not too old to make a comeback even as a matador, you know!"

Pacote answered brusquely so as to end this conversation as mercifully as possible. "No, I'm sorry, man."

"I'm a good man with the sticks, Paco, you know how they used to call me."

"No," said Pacote. "I'm sorry."

Cayetano nodded, as though he'd never really expected the job and didn't blame Pacote for refusing. He looked around the ornate room. His bloodshot eyes studied the things on the desk as intently as though they were in a museum showcase. There was the old framed photo of

Pacote's mother and father standing uncomfortably in front of a painted pastoral backdrop. On the other end of the desk was the photo of Pacote and Socorro taken at the Stork Club when they had stopped in New York for a week on the way back from Mexico. There was the wallet with all the bull brands mounted on it in gold — a present from General Franco three years ago for having dedicated the second bull of the La Prensa corrida to him. There was the doll, a little spangled bullfighter with a fairly accurate caricature of Pacote's sad face, and the cigarette case made from a bull's cojones — you could tell because there was no seam in the two parts that slid together.

He started to go. Then he saw Chaves's wig on the floor. He stooped down and picked it up.

"Y eso?" he mumbled stupidly. "And this?"

"Una peluca," said Chaves with a gentle grin. "Put it on — you need it worse than me."

Cayetano looked at it dully as he turned it over in his hands. Then he stood in front of the full-length mirror on the closet door. With his pudgy fingers he put the wig on his head very solemnly. It made him look funny, but it took twenty years off him. A silence came over the room as he stared transfixed at his reflection. He was unconscious of the people in the room. He squared his shoulders and sucked in his stomach. He raised his head to make his double chin disappear. His eyes narrowed, and his mouth eased into the arrogant sneer that a matador affects when going out to meet the bull. His right arm came forward slightly as though holding a muleta and a sword. It wasn't hard to imagine him striding out into the arena in Madrid the day of his presentation, handsome and lithe, and with thirty thousand people screaming how they loved him.

He looked at one profile, and then the other. He was lost in another generation for a few minutes. Then reluctantly he took the wig off and put it on the dresser.

The sag came back in his body, the stoop in his shoulders, and without saying anything, he shuffled out the door.

The men remained uncomfortably silent. Then Pacote sighed and said "Aí!" between clenched teeth and went to the telephone.

"Oiga, conserje," he said. "Niño de Ronda will be just going through the lobby. Tell him I was wrong. We do need a man today. Have him be at the plaza at ten minutes to four. And sober."

He hung up and avoided looking at Chaves.

"You're a fool," said Chaves, as though stating a long-accepted fact.

2

MATAGATOS glanced at his watch and stood up. "Well, I'd better get over to the sorteo."

"Wait till I get dressed," said Pacote. "I'm coming too."

"To the sorteo?" Chaves exclaimed.

"You've never done that," Matagatos said, almost critically.

"I want to take a look at them today." Pacote stripped off his pajamas. A jagged scar ran across the top of his bony chest, a chest that was broad but tubercular-thin. "Going to draw them myself today. For luck."

"Might be for bad luck, Paco. You've never drawn for yourself."

"No, it'll be for good luck today." He pulled on a pair of gray flannels.

To hell with this luck business. He knew that Chaves knew that he couldn't stand not seeing what was going to try to kill him in the last fight of his life.

He went into the big tiled bathroom, before putting on his shirt, and brushed his teeth.

"I forgot to tell you," Chaves called to him. "There's a toothpaste out called 'Crema de Dientes Pacote.' Didn't even ask our permission. We could sue them."

Pacote washed his face and ran his hand over the slight bluish-green stubble that was only on his upper lip and the right side of his chin. It didn't grow around the two-inch scar that notched the left side. It was Belmonte, el gran Juan, who said that the beard grew more on the day of a corrida, that Fear made it grow more.

He looked at his hands. I'll wait and shave later, he thought. I'll be steadier after I see the cattle. Besides, it will be better to be as recently and well shaved as possible for this last one. Best to be as little ugly as possible today.

"It's red, too," Chaves said. "Can you imagine brushing your teeth with red stuff? You'd think you were spitting blood all the time."

God, you are ugly, Pacote thought as he looked in the mirror and combed his hair. Uglier than the sea. A gray — almost white — streak went down the middle of it. There was no gray on the sides, but down the middle was the streak that looked like a misplaced highlight. It had only started to appear a couple of years ago, and it was getting whiter all the time.

"I could find out the name of the company that makes that stuff," Chaves said as Pacote came out of the bathroom and put on his shirt. "We ought to get a percentage at least, same way we do on Anís Pacote. Except nobody's going to buy red toothpaste. Who wants to think he's spitting blood every morning?"

Matagatos picked up the phone. "I'll get el Buick." He pronounced it "bweek."

"We'll walk," said Pacote. "It's only a few blocks."

"You don't want to get tired, chico," said Chaves. It occurred to him to scratch his groin.

"I was born tired," Pacote said.

"Compadre better stay here," said Matagatos. "He'll bark at the cattle."

"No, he won't," said Pacote. He was feeling better now. Calmer. "Ven, Compadre!" The old dog jumped stiffly off the bed and followed them condescendingly.

As they went out the door Pacote grabbed the wig and plopped it backwards on Chaves's shiny dome.

"Que lindo eres," he said. "How beautiful you are. And so well dressed." Scabs of food on the lapels and archipelagos of grease spots always graced Chaves's sport coats.

"Son of the great whore," Pepe muttered.

The drought caused electricity restrictions, and the elevator didn't work until one, so the three men walked down the heavily carpeted stairs. When they came into the tiled lobby two people — obviously Americans — were talking to the conserje.

"Perdón, Matador," said the conserje, coming out from behind the counter. "But this journalist would like to meet you. He is with a big American magazine. He says he's going to do an article on you." He brought them over.

The man, thirty and handsome in a crew-cut eager, undergraduate sort of way, advanced. "My name's Newton, Señor Pacote." They shook hands. "And this is my wife, Helen." He nodded pleasantly at Chaves and Mata-gatos. He had a good smile, in spite of the fact that two of his front teeth almost crossed over each other.

The woman wore a mink stole over her black dress, a little mink hat perched on her dark upswept hair, and harlequin dark glasses. She looked socially prominent, but the type of society woman that could be easily induced to lend her name and face to a cold-cream advertisement.

"I wonder if I could get a couple." Newton held up the Leica that hung from a strap around his neck.

"Ah, una foto," Pacote said aloofly but politely. Here was the audience. He slipped into the part of the tranquil, fearless matador, and the feigned calm brought him genuine calm. "You are aficionados?"

"Sí, mucho," said the man. "Muy aficionados. We came down here from Paris especially for the fight today. I'm doing an article on it for my magazine. Helen here is crazy about the sport, worse than I am." He tapped his head with a forefinger. "Un poquito loca en el coco por los toros."

"It's the greatest thing in the world," the woman said, with fierce sincerity. Like her husband, she spoke fluent Spanish.

"We saw you last year in Mexico City," said the man. "You and Silverio. Paid fifty dollars for rotten seats but glad to get them. It was the most tremendous emotional experience I ever had in my life, and I've been wanting to do an article on you ever since. I didn't even know anything about it then. It was my second fight and I didn't know anything — still thought the bulls charged because the cape was red."

"No," said Pacote. "You're right, they're color-blind."

Chaves held his wrist up and tapped the watch.

"I must go," Pacote began, "We . . ."

"Oh no, please," said Newton. "The photo. Outside."

They went out into the bright sun of the driveway in front of the hotel. Newton walked ahead and turned around peering through the camera. Pacote stood there, a little ill at ease, as Newton held the light meter on him. A man going by with a side of beef slung over his shoulder stopped to watch. Chaves and Matagatos stepped aside out of range of the camera, and the little dog followed them.

"I'm hardly the autograph-hound type," said the woman with a self-deprecating laugh, "and I've never done anything like this before, but would you mind if I stood with you in the photo?"

"Encantado," said Pacote. "Charmed."

Newton took three pictures. "Would you mind smiling, señor?"

A hint of a shy smile hovered in one corner of Pacote's mouth. "On fight days I'm too scared to smile."

"Please smile," coaxed the woman. "A bigger smile."

Pacote's mouth widened a little, cautiously, like a woman afraid to crack her mudpack, and Newton took the picture. Then they shook hands and said good-bye.

"Lots of luck," said Newton. "We're going to see a great day today. Something we'll tell our grandchildren about."

"I don't know," said Pacote. And his calm suddenly left him. "We'll do what we can." He snapped his fingers for the dog. "Come on, Compadre."

"Good luck," Newton called after them. "I'd like to talk to you later about an interview."

"That," breathed Helen Newton, as she watched Pacote stride out of sight, "is the most attractive man in the world."

3

THE THREE MEN were down by the river now, walking past the round, squat Tower of Gold where Columbus stored his treasures after a voyage. "We can just bury that hay, Paco."

"What hay?"

"That hay about I don't know, we'll do what we can. You're going to coast this afternoon. Nobody'll blame you. Don't get any ideas about giving those Yanquis and all the rest of the blood-drinking goats one last great afternoon. You've given them a hundred other great afternoons they can damn well remember."

"I'm not going to do anything today," said Pacote. "Coast all the way."

"Well, don't forget it after you get in the ring. Tano is going to be out to commit suicide to make you look bad. Don't lose your head. Let him cut ears if he wants to. You just get out whole. We'll have a good party afterward. Have all the newspapermen over and cut the pigtail. It'll be a great party."

"I'm not going to lose my head."

In front of one of the little open bodega bars was one of the huge posters advertising the fight, and Pacote's heart skipped a little as he saw it. It was always terrifying to see it in big print, something so irrevocable about it when the posters were actually up.

"The taurine event of the decade," the words shouted; "4 toros bravos de Miura 4." Then came his name and Tano's in letters five inches high. Up above the names was a gaudy painting by Ruano Llopis. In hot yellows and reds it depicted a life-size Pacote executing a muletazo, the bull charging straight out at the viewer.

"I've always liked that one," said Chaves.

"I'd like it better if it had your name underneath," said Pacote.

A man in a beret and dungarees standing at the bar in front of great barrels of manzanilla spotted him.

"Pacote!" he exclaimed. He came out proffering a large glass of cognac and some red crayfish on a tray. "Don Paco, do me the honor of taking a copitiya."

"Coñac, no — muchas gracias," Pacote said hesitantly to his urgings. But God, how he wanted the liquor. "I will take a cigala, though." He wanted ten glasses of cognac like that one. He needed a great bowl of it.

"We must find a female, matador." He ran his finger down the underside of the crayfishes' tails: "Ah, here's one with no spines. The females are more tender."

Pacote suddenly reached out to the tray and took the glass of cognac. "I think I will have . . ."

"No, Paco," Chaves ordered sternly.

"One's not going to hurt me," snapped Pacote, and he

threw the amber liquid down his throat in two gulps. Then he took a crayfish, murmuring, "Very grateful."

"Ni na ni na ni na!" said the man. "After all the emotion you've given me in your day, I should give you a million cigalas and a reservoir of coñac. And we will all be there in the first row of the sun-and-shade section to ovation you this afternoon."

Pacote said good-bye and moved on. He husked off the shell of the crayfish as he walked and put the white meat in his mouth absently. *In your day*, his brain kept saying, *in your day!* He tossed the claws and the head of the cigala into the gutter. God, what a feeling that gave you when you heard it for the first time. But the cognac felt good in his stomach and loosened the fear knot a little. If only he had another glass, another big glass of friendly, burning cognac like that one! Just one or two more and then he wouldn't be afraid of anything! But that was suicide.

They walked along by the river and the warm air was good in the lungs, in spite of the fruity smells that came off the sluggish water. Across there was Triana, the gypsy quarter, a colony of dirty houses in narrow streets where baskets and pottery were made, and sad songs were wailed and where the young gitanos sneaked out to the ranches to fight the bulls by moonlight and dreamed of someday being The Best, like Pacote Torres.

A fancy wagon came toward them, pulled by four perfectly matched mules with gay headresses wagging and pompons on the harness bouncing. A coachman in a broad-brimmed hat and the short jacket of the Andaluz costume sat on the box, but a handsome mustached man in a business suit and a Homburg hat was driving.

"Don Eduardo," said Matagatos.

He pulled up the reins in his gloved hands and greeted them cheerily.

"Hola," said Pacote. Eduardo was all right. He didn't know much about the business his great-grandfather had founded, but he was a good type.

"We'll see a great day, Paco," Eduardo said, "I've sent the four best on the ranch. All good. Brought them in from Tablada early this morning. Go take a look at them. Lots of luck." He waved and drove on.

Christ, how can anyone be cheery today, Pacote thought. And then his mind flashed back to *in your day!*

"Good!" exclaimed Matagatos. "No such thing as a good Miura."

"Eduardo sure as hell better have sent a good corrida," said Chaves. "I still think we should have gone to the ranch and picked them ourselves. Only way you can be sure they're going to be like *that*" — he held out his hand at great Dane height — " and like *this*" — he made a pair of turned-in horns out of his thumb and forefinger. "Modern bullfighting, my friend, is based on the principle of the big bill in the wallet and the little bull in the arena."

"And have Tano saying I wouldn't have fought unless I had goats? This last one has to be done right, chico, you know that. He's always said I was afraid of Miuras. Sure, I'm afraid of anything with horns. I don't even like snails."

They came to the ring, the Maestranza, the beautiful Maestranza, second oldest plaza de toros in Spain. The great stone pillars and the majestic arch of the threatening coliseum had glowered out at the river like this for two centuries. How still and cruel it seemed now, an empty shell of cruelty, stark and stripped of the screaming people and the brass band. How many men like me, thought Pacote, how many cowards like me have passed by here the morning of the fight and felt their guts contract with fear at the nakedness of the arena and the nakedness inside their bodies? Maybe there were one or two in the two hundred years who were as afraid. Surely there must have been one as afraid.

He saw a man plastering a big poster on the side of the ring announcing the novillada of next Sunday. All new kids. Well, today could be worse, Pacote thought. It could be the beginning instead of the end.

They turned down the side street to where the high corral wall jutted out from the plaza. There were a lot of urchins hanging around a large wooden door and several beggars and a gypsy shoeshine man. Chaves banged on it twice. It opened cautiously first and then all the way when the gatekeeper saw who it was. They stepped in the little sunny patio, where several men were gathered in knots smoking and talking. They were banderilleros, picadors, ex-bullfighters, promoters, newspapermen, gentlemen aficionados, and hangers-on. They stopped talking and looked at Pacote, hoping to get a nod or a wave from The Best.

The foreman in charge of the bulls came up to them. He was dressed in the big-brimmed Cordobés hat and the short bolero jacket of the Andaluz rancher.

"Hola, Matador," he said in his friendly, respectful Andaluz accent. "You are drawing them yourself, I see. Tano's man is up there already. The dog won't bark at the cattle, will he?"

"No. He's a good dog."

They went up the stone steps to the top of the corral. The walls were wide and an iron railing ran around on both sides. Several men were up there looking down at the bulls, talking softly and occasionally pointing at one or another of the animals. One of them was Tano's banderillero. A large faded sign stenciled on the corral wall warned: "It is strictly prohibited to talk at the cattle or molest them."

Pacote knew everyone was watching him, and he didn't want them to know how anxious he was to see the bulls. He didn't look down. He made himself walk over to Tano's man first.

"Buenos días," he said.

"Buenos días," said the banderillero a little coldly. "What do you think of the oxen?"

"I haven't seen them yet," Pacote replied casually. Then he turned slowly and looked down in the corral.

It was a relief to see them, for the unknown was worse than reality no matter how bad. His eyes skipped from one to the other of the animals milling quietly together, taking them all in quickly, and then going back to study them individually. All four of them were solid black, fairly uniform of horn and not too big. They never looked big from up above, but God, how they grew when you found yourself on their level in the ring!

He turned to Chaves. "Pepe?" he asked, and he awaited the answer tensely, for no one in the world knew so much about bulls as José "Pepe" Chaves. Some people claimed he could tell how a bull would fight just by watching it a while in the corrals, how many times it would charge the pics, and whether it would fight a brave or defensive fight. Pacote knew that Pepe Chaves could have become the greatest bullfighter who had ever lived; at twenty he had had the build and knew so much about bulls that they said he could talk bull language. But he was a coward. He couldn't keep his feet from dancing away from the horns no matter how hard he tried, so he "cut the pigtail," and took to managing men who were braver than he.

Chaves didn't answer. He took off his dark glasses and studied the animals carefully. Then he pulled the corners of his mouth down exaggeratedly and wagged one hand, thumb extended, like an airplane signaling. So-so. He put his glasses back on.

"They look very even to me," said Pacote, trying to keep the anxiety out of his voice. "They look good." It was as though he could make the bulls better by wheedling Pepe into saying they were good.

"Regular," said Pepe. He always scratched the back of his left hand with his right fingers when he was concentrating hard. "Neither foo nor fa. But they're all right."

And Pacote knew him well enough to know he meant it, that he wasn't just trying to make him feel good. Pepe was usually a bit on the pessimistic side, too. He began to feel a little more confidence seeing the bulls now and hearing Chaves say that they were all right. The fear organ was still there big in his chest, but it wasn't strangling him. It was good to see the animals. When you just stayed in your hotel room you imagined them as strange monsters, not really bulls, but weird, black-bloody shapes, that could blur and become unicorns or dinosaurs. It was good to see that they were just bulls, bulls like the hundreds of others he had killed in his life. Only he wasn't the same person who had killed all the others, the one thousand and three others. Before, it was the beginning and the drive of young, hot ambition. And then it was the middle part with confidence and the surety that you were The Best. But now it was the end, and there was doubt and fear, and the

timing was going fast like a handful of water dribbling out of the cupped palms through the fingers.

"Let's get them paired off," Tano's banderillero was saying.

Two of the bulls were clearly "better" than the others. They were the smallest, and their horns turned in a little, but not too much. And one of these was better, smaller and prettier, with "a comfortable head." A real "nun." Tano's banderillero wrote the numbers of the big scraggly white brands on their sides on two separate pieces of cigarette paper.

Chaves clapped his hands together twice, grunting,

"Huh, toro!" The bulls snorted and raised their heads and shook their horns aggressively. Number one hundred and twenty stepped back, dropping his head very low and pawing the earth. Chaves began to whistle softly to himself some urgent, nameless tune. He didn't purse his lips; his mouth merely assumed a strangely prissy look and the air came out from no visible opening.

Finally he said: "Number one-twenty looks a little manso to me." Manso means tame, and a tame bull is a cowardly and dangerous one. "Course, you can't tell till he gets in the ring, but I have that feeling."

"All right," said Tano's banderillero unquestioningly; Chaves's hunches were famous. "We'll put him here" — he wrote the number on one paper — "and the bigger one with the spread we'll put here. The nun goes with one-twenty."

The papers were crumpled up and dropped into the broad-brimmed hat of the foreman. Pacote gave a suggestion of a bow and extended his hand in a you-first gesture.

"After you, Mata'or," said the banderillero grudgingly.

Pacote reached in, felt a paper, and drew it halfway out. Then he dropped it, and took the other one and unfolded it. He had not drawn 120. Maybe today would be a lucky day after all. He showed the paper to Pepe.

"I'm glad neither of us is fighting the sobrero," said the banderillero. He jerked his thumb toward the other corral. Pacote and Chaves walked along the wall and looked down. The bull was alone. It was a substitute bull, in case one of the others broke a horn or wouldn't charge the horses or was blind in one eye or limped. It looked up at them and pawed the dust.

"That is a bull?" snorted Chaves. "They have crossed an elephant with a gnu." The animal was a pinto, black and white, with uneven and twisted horns. It was gigantic. "What an uncle. If you ever got hooked on the right corkscrew you'd never get off. A real ox."

"And his name is Pocapena," said Tano's banderillero with a laugh. "Señor Not-Much-Trouble. Like the one that made cold cuts of Granero in Madrid."

"I'm glad today's my last," said Pacote. "With my luck, I would draw that cathedral as a regular in some other fight."

They arranged the order that the bulls would be fought. Then they shook hands with several people and left.

As they went out the big door, a black Fiat pulled up and a chauffeur emerged to open the rear door. Out stepped a little mushroom of a man in a brown felt hat with the brim turned down all the way around. It was Juan Belmonte, the father of modern bullfighting and brother of Manolo Belmonte, "empresario" of the Maestranza.

4

"HO-*la!*" Belmonte exclaimed with his big jaw out and a chuckle in his voice. "Look who we have here."

"Don Juan," Pacote said and they shook hands. Though he was only fifty-five, everyone always put the "Don" in front of Belmonte's name — even his contemporaries and older matadors like El Gallo who knew him intimately. There was nothing about him that demanded respect; he was just automatically accorded it.

"Matador, are you acquainted with this ball of suet at your left?" Belmonte said, holding Pacote's hand in both of his and pretending to ignore Chaves. "I hadn't heard he'd been released from the penitentiary."

"They've released him in my custody," said Pacote. "But I have to guarantee that he doesn't molest pregnant women and doesn't throw any more bottles in church."

"Osú, que miedo!" said Belmonte, shaking his head. "Jesus, what fear! An unenviable task."

Chaves grunted with pleasure and shook hands with Belmonte.

"How goes the cattle, Pepe?" Belmonte asked. As he talked he ran his finger over the vague hint of a mustache on his upper lip. For a reason known only to himself, he grew a thin mustache every Lenten period, and he hadn't got around to shaving it off this year.

Chaves wagged his hand again. "Regular. Not bad."

"They had better be not bad, or we'll put young Señor Miura in an iron maiden, eh? A real Inquisition, eh?"

This could be me someday, Pacote was thinking, as he'd thought so many times before. Belmonte was the exception, he was the opposite of Niño de Ronda. Long since retired, he was around to enjoy the immortality that he had sweated and shed so much blood to obtain. Here was the man who, because of his imagination and skill and guts and physical limitations, had changed bullfighting from the brute act of butchering a bull into a beautiful science. And, yet here he was still alive, proof that it could be done. It was good to see him, the proof, at this moment. The other man who hadn't been content with mere greatness but who shot for immortality, the gypsy Joselito, the man of whom they said there was no heifer who could drop the bull that could kill him, had his charmed life ripped out of him in 1920, when he was only twenty-four, by a scrawny, treacherous substitute bull in Talavera de la Reina. Now he lay on the other side of Sevilla under a huge tomb depicting nineteen life-size figures bearing his coffin, and every May 16, ceremonies were held at his grave and the newspapers published pictures of him and famous poets wrote dirges and odes to him and there were statues of him in wax museums. That's what they'd do with Pacote if he were to get it; immortalize him. But to hell with the nothingness of that kind of immortality! He wanted all of what Belmonte had — the health, respect, intelligent friends, the sun of the large estate, the fine ranch that sent out at least six corridas and two novilladas a season, the wife, the sons and daughters, the grandchildren. But he didn't want his son to be a bullfighter, like Belmonte's. He should be a . . .

"Matador?" Belmonte was offering him a pencil-thin cigar. Pacote didn't like cigars, but he took it; it was good, it was luck, to receive something from Belmonte now. He lit it eagerly, as though in the smoking of this object that had belonged to the Earthquake from Triana he might inhale some of the man's invulnerability.

"They're saying over at the Gallango that you're making another comeback," said Chaves, his fingers twirling the cigar in his lips and the other hand holding his lighter to the end like a glass blower. "They say Madrid's offered you four hundred thousand pesetas for a comeback fight."

"Osú, que miedo!" Belmonte's head went back and his jaw jutted out like a barracuda as the noises he called laughing came out. "Jesus, what fear! Four hundred thousand pesetas is what I would offer to anyone able to put me in condiciones físicas to be able to fight again! No, chicos, now I go back to the ring only like today, to sit in the box of the presidente of the ring."

"You're advising today?"

"Yes, I asked for it. El Gallo and I. We want to give the baby here a good sendoff. Well, I'd better go take a look at the cattle if I'm going to see them before they go into the stalls."

Pacote didn't want him to leave, as though he might learn the secret of survival from this man who had retired three times, who had fought three "last" corridas. But he could think of nothing more to say to keep him and they shook hands. Belmonte said undramatically, but looking hard into Pacote's eyes, "The danger in a last fight is not in the cattle, boy. It's in oneself. The crowd suddenly seems very loving and tolerant, and you forget the beast it has been in the past. One is tempted to, you know, to give them a sort of bonus or a reminder of one's greatness."

"I feel no such urge," said Pacote with a wry smile, "I assure you."

"Not now you don't," said Belmonte. He fumbled in his pocket and brought out a little worn silver medallion. "Look, boy, I'm neither one of those superstitious ones nor the highly religious ones, but I had this thing with me when I fought my retirement fights. As I say, I'm not much of a man for relics and such, but it would do no harm for you to wear it. I was going to bring it up to you at the hotel when you were dressing, but now I won't bother to go."

Pacote took the little medal gratefully and put it in his pocket. "Gracias, Don Juan. Gracias."

"It will bring you luck. Training and skill are fine, but a little luck . . ." Belmonte smiled, "that's a good thing to have, too."

Then there was no more to say, and they shook hands again, and Belmonte turned and went into the corrals.

As they walked back along the river, Pacote said: "What are you going to do, Pepe?"

"When?"

"After." They'd discussed it before, but he wanted to talk, to get his mind off the bulls.

"Find some half-assed kind," said Chaves, fanning his sweaty fat face with his wig. "Make a torero out of bull fodder, like I did you. And you, you'll be loafing around Córdoba breeding cathedrals with sabers to hurt my kid."

Pacote put his hand in his pocket. He felt Belmonte's medallion and it was good to finger it. Wonderful to feel it. "Pepe, I'm going to make that ranch really beautiful. It's going to have a parlor like nothing you ever saw. Nobody in my family ever had a house with a parlor. I always dreamed of the one I'd have when I had the money. It'll have big red plush curtains, see, and a thick carpet, so thick you actually feel yourself sink in it, and potted plants around and tiles set in the wall. You'll come up, and after a wonderful dinner of gazpacho and paella we'll sit around in the parlor and drink and talk. Then we'll ride around and look at the calves. Or we can go out and watch the fish jump. I'm going to put fish in the pond, not to catch them but just to watch them jump in the evening." He walked along silently for a while, warm in the wonderful scenes he could imagine in such detail but couldn't describe. Then he said: "Why don't you come be my mayoral, chico?" He could feel the bas-relief of the little Virgin. His fingers clutched it convulsively. "I'm going to raise the best damn bulls in Spain. God knows we have the money to do it."

Chaves grinned. "I like the stink of the rings too much, chico. When I hear the olés they're for me too. But I'll help you set it up."

"Don't you ever want to get married? You a maricón or something?"

"I been married."

"Owl droppings!" Pacote exclaimed.

"No, really, I was married. I was fished when I was twenty. Caught by the sash."

"Now I know Christ is coming again. What was she — a three-year-old Miura?"

"She was a gypsy from Triana, una gitana legítima. And she was young, and prettier than the sea, and I was on top of the world after my début fight in Madrid. I wanted her more than I ever wanted anything in my life. But she wouldn't give it to me. She said she wanted to get married. So I said all right, we'll be married. So we had a ceremony in my hotel room. My banderilleros were the witnesses and my picador came in with his collar turned around and mumbled what he thought sounded like Latin and he made a fine fat priest. I guess — God, I can't even remember her name — I guess she wasn't too bright, because . . ."

"You know what they say: Talk about the miracle all you want, but don't mention the saint's name."

"Well, anyway, she didn't catch on and — Lola, that's it! That was her name — and she thought we were really married. After the ceremony the priest and the witnesses got out, and Lola and I were just about to — how do they call it in books — consummate the union? — when her brothers and her father broke into the room. They were big and I was little and they had knives and I didn't, and they marched me over to Triana and married us again. You ought to see a gypsy wedding. It takes three days. Four months later I caught her catting around, and I left her and then when" . . .

Pacote stopped and said abruptly: "Pepe."

Chaves grunted inquisitively at the different tone in Pacote's voice.

"Pepe, I've been thinking about that will."

Chaves threw his cigar away. "That's a hell of a thing to be thinking about!"

"No, I was just thinking maybe I should have mentioned Matagatos and Cascabel somewhere along the line instead of just dumping it all on my mother and telling her to take care of them."

"That's a hell of a thing to be thinking about." He put his hand on Pacote's shoulder roughly. "Let's just skip that, eh? We'll talk about it tomorrow."

The nervous anger came suddenly. "All right," he rasped. "Now tell me the truth, god damn it, tell me what you really think of the Miuras!"

"I told you, Pacote," said Chaves quietly. "They're all right."

Pacote caught him by the lapels. "You swear it? You're not handing me manure?"

"We've never operated that way, chico."

Pacote released the other's coat. "No," he said contritely, "we've never operated that way." They started walking again.

As they went by the Tower of Gold, they saw two ragged boys playing at bullfighting. One, a skinny ten-year-old with a shaved head, had a gunny sack spread over a wooden sword which he shook at the other boy, grunting professionally: "Huh, toro, huh!" The bull, crouched over and holding a pair of slaughterhouse horns in front of him, pawed the ground and then charged.

"Me," said Pacote thoughtfully as he stopped to watch.

"And me," said Chaves.

The "matador" now held the sack differently, reaching around in back of him to grasp the cloth by the corner. It was the pacotina pass. Again the bull charged.

"Olé," Chaves called. "But watch that animal, he has a terrible hook."

The boys stopped and stared at the men open-mouthed. "Pacote!" gasped the "matador." He looked as though he might almost drop to his knees in reverence.

"Sí, chiquillo," said Chaves grinning, "and if you're going to be like him, and if I'm going to manage you, you'll have to keep your knees stiffer and run your arm more."

Pacote had seen hundreds of boys at this game, but for some reason the grimy faces and bare feet and the professional way the skinny one had worked his mouth and frowned as he cited the bull moved him profoundly. Suddenly he took out his wallet and pulled out all the money in it.

"Here," he said and slapped the five thousand pesetas into the "matador's" filthy hand. "Divide it."

He walked on, leaving the boy staring dumbly after him, the bills fluttering off the unclosed hand to the ground.

"The man's out of his mind," muttered Chaves to himself, as he hustled to keep up.

"For luck," said Pacote. "And for God's sake, remind me to clip this medallion on my chain before the fight."

5

WHEN THEY CAME into the hotel lobby they saw a group of newspapermen lounging around the tiled fountain in the patio. They hurried up to Pacote and a photographer snapped a picture as he strode to the elevator.

"How about a statement, Matador?" one of them called.

"Anything," said another, "just something about how you feel, anything."

"What do you think of Tano Ruiz?" asked another. "How are the Miuras?"

One was the American, and he said, "Please, Señor Pacote, could I talk to you in your room?"

But Chaves elbowed them aside and kept walking. "Have some kindness, señores," he growled. "A little kindness. After the fight Paco will talk all you want."

They stepped into the elevator and the grill slid across to bar the reporters.

When they got up to the room, Suárez, the monkey-faced sword boy, was there stripping the white protective covers off a green and silver uniform and laying it out on

45

the chair. He was no boy but a fifty-year-old man, and he had been with Pacote for ten years. His hair was cut short, and he looked like one of those grinning clay heads that one puts seeds in to grow grass hair.

"Good day, Mata'or," said the little man, brushing a finger by his head in a salute. "I took the liberty of ordering lunch for you."

"Put that one away." This was terribly important. "I want the white and gold." It was three years old, but he'd had luck wearing it. "Hola, old one," he said as an afterthought, rubbing his hand over Suárez's cropped head affectionately.

There was a tray on the desk with a thin steak still steaming with the olive oil it was cooked in, a potato omelet, and a pot of coffee. Pacote took the coffee and drank it sitting on the edge of the bed.

"You better eat something," said Chaves, handing him the plate with the steak. "You'll be weak otherwise."

"And if I get a horn in me?"

"You're not going to be operated on today. You're not going within three feet of them. Eat!"

Pacote cut a piece of steak, but halfway to his mouth he stopped the fork and put it down on the plate. He cut the meat into small pieces very precisely and then gave it to the dog and pushed the tray away.

Chaves looked at him sharply, but didn't say anything. Then he stood up abruptly and pulled the shades. "It's one-thirty, chico. Get some sleep."

"Where you going?" asked Pacote.

"I've got something to do," said Pepe uneasily.

"What?" asked Pacote.

"Just something."

Pacote looked at him suspiciously. Then, as Chaves started to go, he said: "Listen, I've been thinking about Niño de Ronda. He could mess up everything. Get us all killed. Maybe we ought to get someone else."

"He's all right." Chaves's eyes wandered to the partly-filled whiskey bottle on the dresser. But they didn't really wander; it was as though that bottle with the staid label printed like a government bond had been bothering him for some time. "He's not that bad. Get some sleep. I'll be in my room in about half an hour if you want anything."

The sword boy went out, and Chaves started to follow. Then he swung around and grabbed the bottle and clumsily tucked it under his coat.

"For a friend of mine," he mumbled, and went out the door without looking at Pacote.

The great protective Pepe, Pacote said to himself. Well for God's sake, I wasn't going to drink it. Maybe I'm a little shot, but I'm not crazy yet.

He took off his clothes and climbed into the bed which hadn't been made yet. He fell into a fitful sleep almost immediately.

He woke up knowing someone had slipped into the dark-ened room. Then he heard Compadre's belated growl.

"Who is it?" he asked, sitting up, the clock in his head telling him that it was too early for Chaves or Suárez to be coming to get him ready.

"Me," said a voice, and he knew it was the American.

"What do you want?" Pacote asked, but not gruffly, almost eagerly, glad to have been taken away from his nightmares.

"To talk to you if I could," said Newton. "I should have interviewed you earlier today before all those others came around. I had a hell of a time getting up here away from them."

Pacote turned on the light and stuffed the pillow behind him. It was nice and cool on the side he hadn't been lying on. For a second there was a flash as though he'd spent all his adult life in bed stuffing a pillow behind him to semi-sit up so that someone who was entirely safe and would always be safe could ask him questions.

"Would you like a drink?" he asked.

"All right," Newton said. "Sure, I'd like one. Sorry about barging in like this, but this story's very important to me."

"On the dresser," said Pacote.

"Will you have one?"

"I have to fight today."

"And you mean you can't drink before a performance? I should think you'd want a little shot or two for your nerves. I should think it would make you braver."

"We have a saying — a man can get very drunk, but he never gets so drunk he eats a live coal."

"Good quote. But I'd think it would make you more inventive, too, having a drink or two."

"A drunk tightrope walker could probably think up a lot of fine tricks that way too." Pacote reached for a cigarette from the bed table and lit it. "But he'd fall off the wire before he could do them."

"So bullfighters never drink before a performance?"

"Not unless they're bored with breathing."

Newton made a note on a piece of paper folded in his wallet. Then he went to the dresser. "I don't see any bottle."

That's right. The Great Protector had taken it.

"There is one in the top drawer."

Newton took the bottle out and poured the drink. Then he came over and sat in a chair by the bed.

"Salud y pesetas." He held up his drink. "Health and wealth."

"And love without a mother-in-law," Pacote answered automatically.

"That's a new one."

"No, it's old," he said. He watched Newton drink, yearning for some of the amber fear medicine.

"Do you speak English?"

"Oh yes, very well," said Pacote, blowing out smoke through his nose. "I can say 'ow moch yew charch fer dat fairy fine ombrella!"

"That's fine," Newton grinned. "Where did you learn that?"

"I don't know. A book, I think." He made himself look away from the man's half-empty glass.

"Do you mind my being here?" Newton asked. "I've got some questions I'd sure like to ask you."

"I have to fight soon."

"I never in my life went through anything like that time we saw you in Mexico. I didn't realize that just a man and a red cloth and a bull could, you know — sort of transport a person." Newton drank again, and Pacote watched the liquid go down his throat. "Please don't do anything like that today. I couldn't take it twice."

Pacote managed a grim smile. "Don't worry, señor."

"No, I was just joking. I guess you just *have* to be great today. After all, people have come from all over the world just to see it." Newton took out his paper and pencil again. "One thing I wanted to know is why you never smile in the ring like the other fighters."

"It's a very serious thing, this thing of the bulls."

"You know, we saw you once in America, in the Stork Club. You and your wife. It was a few months ago."

"Oh?"

"Yes. Is your wife here with you?"

"I'm not married."

"Your sweetheart?"

"Something like that."

"She here?"

"She's in Granada."

"How come she's not here?"

Pacote didn't answer. This American's questions were beginning to irritate him. But he didn't want him to go and leave him alone.

"I've relived that performance we saw in Mexico a thousand times in my mind. I just hope today's that good. The grace, the ballet of it. That pass with the cape you do, you know, the verónica. It's just like a dance step. The whole thing is just a terrific ballet."

"Just a ballet," Pacote said. His irritation was building. "But if you make a mistake you pay for it with an autopsy."

Newton looked at the scar on Pacote's chest. "Have you had many wounds?"

"I've been pretty lucky."

"How many though? Sorry to have to pump you this way but I've got to get all this information."

"My share." God, how to shut him up?

"A few perhaps?"

"Perhaps."

"I've heard a rumor that the reason you fight so suicidally is that you've got T.B. and don't care about living anyway — that isn't true is it?"

Pacote shook his head. "They've said that for years. I had pneumonia when I was young. That's all. I'm no Tarzán, but I'm all right." He pronounced it Tah*thann*. Then he added "And I care a lot about living, my friend."

"What does it feel like to have a horn go in you? What do you think about while it's happening?"

"Listen," Pacote said. Anything to get him off this talk. "I think — think I'll change my mind. Would you make me a drink? A weak one."

"Sure, I wouldn't think one would hurt you. It'll calm you down."

He made the drink for him and another one for himself.

"No, listen," Pacote said hastily. "I can't. Throw it out."

"I should think it would calm you down. I always used to have a couple of shots before I boxed at college." He handed him the glass.

"This doesn't look so weak," Pacote said. "You'd better throw it out. It looks strong."

"Well, I always say good whiskey doesn't need water and bad whiskey doesn't deserve it."

Pacote regarded the glass warily, but then he drank. He savoured it gratefully.

"What *does* it feel like?" Newton persisted.

"It feels good," he said looking at his glass and knowing the man didn't mean the drink.

"No, I mean getting gored."

"Well, it feels as though you were on a very hard and sharp horn, and you wish sincerely that you were off of it. Or that you had gone into cabinetmaking, the way your mother had hoped you would."

"Your mother wanted you to be a carpenter?"

"My mother wanted me to be a carpenter or a pimp or a burglar or a typhoid carrier or anything that didn't have to do with bulls." He suddenly had to talk. It was easier to talk with the whiskey glass in his hand. "She was married to a bullfighter who was killed. Fuentes. Maybe you've heard of him. Then she married my father, and he was a pretty good fighter — not too good, I guess, but pretty good — and he began to go blind. He stayed in the game as long as he could distinguish the shape of the bull — sometimes he saw two bulls — you can imagine he took a lot of punishment — and then he died in the poorhouse. So you can see that the bulls weren't very good to my mother."

"But they've been good to you."

Pacote shrugged. "God says take what you want — but pay for it."

"Aren't you glad you're somebody," Newton said, "something great, and not just a carpenter?"

He drank. "You picked the wrong day to ask me that. Ask me tomorrow."

"I think it's the only thing left in this neon world with any color and chivalry and pageantry. To me you're medieval. You're all like something out of another age. Or mythology. If you wanted to get fancy, you could say the picador is a centaur and the toreador is the god of the dance."

"Torero," Pacote said trying to keep the irritation out of his voice. "There's no such word as toreador."

"There isn't?"

"Only in the song."

Newton had covered one side of his paper with jottings, and he turned it over and folded it the other way.

"Say, how about that streak in your hair? Seems to me you didn't have that in Mexico, or at least not that gray. Doesn't it bother you? Sort of a . . . "

"A reminder of how old and shot I am?" Pacote started to order him from the room, but he drank and took refuge in an aphorism. "Just because there's a little snow on the roof doesn't mean the fire's out in the hearth. Everyone's suddenly treating me like an old man and I'm not even thirty yet!"

Pacote finished his drink, and Newton handed him another.

But Pacote put it down on the bedside table hard. "Listen, I have to fight! In less than two hours."

Newton stood up. "And I better let you get some rest.

Well, I sure appreciate your talking to me, and I hope you have the greatest day of your life today. Lots of luck!"

He went out.

Pacote groaned. He wouldn't get back to sleep now, and he knew it. He finished his drink and the rest of Newton's. He got up and poured another.

As he started to drink it there was a loud knock on the door.

6

PACOTE quickly put the drink in the drawer, but the glass was too tall. The drawer wouldn't close, so he didn't open the door.

"Who is it?" he asked.

"Solórzano," said a coarse voice, "Manuel Solórzano." The heavy Andalu' accent made it "Manway Tholothano."

"Chaves left word for me to come around and see him."

"His room is down the hall," said Pacote, "two-o-seven." He heard the man move away from the door.

Solórzano! So that was it. That's what Pepe had up his sleeve that he didn't want to say anything about. Even Pepe thought he was so completely gone — so helpless — so liable to get killed today — that he had gone out and hired protection, the most butchering, criminal picador in the business!

Pacote took the drink out of the drawer and drained it.

So that's what we've come to! Solórzano, who was hired by Niño de Ronda for his last fights as a matador, when every day he'd have a bull returned to the corral because

he didn't dare get close enough to even stick it in the lungs; Solórzano, without whom the cowardly gypsy Cagancho wouldn't fight; Solórzano, the darling of every ancient re-tired matador doing a benefit fight; Solórzano, indispen-sable to any young kid who'd been pushed too fast and really didn't know how to dominate a bull but just had some superficial filigree stuff. So that's what we've come to. Even Pepe had lost confidence in him. And right now Chaves was talking to this butcher, a jackal Pepe wouldn't spit on ordinarily, talking to him, begging him to protect this poor wreck of a gutless coward!

Pacote put on his Paisley dressing gown quickly and went out into the hall. Chaves's room was only five doors down. When he came near the room he saw the door was open. He heard Chaves's voice. He stopped, and, flattened up against the wall, he listened.

"And so then you'll kill them, eh, Solórzano?" Chaves was obviously eating, for the words could barely find their way out of his mouth. "Bear down on the iron like you've never borne down in your life. Get them in the kidneys, get them in the spine, punish them, get them in the ass, get them in the ribs" — Pacote heard Chaves swallow the mouthful noisily — "just get them. But for God's sake don't cripple them — we don't want to take the chance of getting that substitute bull."

Solórzano grunted. "Easy for you to say. You don't get the cushions. You don't get the Fundador bottles in the back of the head. I got family and a lot of friends in this town. So's my wife. It's no fun to be called a butcher and a son of a whore in front of your friends. Why don't you ask El Pimpi to kill your bulls for you?"

"I'm going to tell him too. But you're heftier and better. You can skin a bull from hump to tail. You can slip in three shots in one charge and leave the bull swaying and begging for the puntilla. I've seen you do it every day when you were working for Cagancho and Niño de Ronda."

"Maybe," said Solórzano, not without some pride in his fame in illegalities. "But I want to look good today."

"Look good!" Chaves exploded. "Who in Christ's name cares whether or not a picador looks good?"

"A picador's family," said Solórzano in an injured tone, "that's who!"

Chaves let out that little mirthless laugh that he always gave when he was trying to control his temper. "Sure, sure. But listen. You realize what an important day this is." He used his persuasive, confidential tone, as though he were talking to a recalcitrant child. "The greatest torero since Joselito is bowing out. Maybe the greatest who ever lived. We got to see he bows out and doesn't get carried out."

"Was," said Solórzano smugly. "Was."

There was a scuffling sound and a grunt as though Chaves had caught Solórzano up by the lapels and jerked the picador's face close to his.

"Listen, you son of the great whore," he hissed, "*is, is, is!* You sister-raping bastard, you aren't fit to be in the same ring with him. The only reason I hired you was because we're in a bad spot and you can butcher a bull dirtier than anybody in the business."

There was a silence and Pacote knew Chaves was working to control himself. Though he'd come to eavesdrop, suddenly he didn't want to hear any more. But he was held there by the savagery of the words he knew would come.

"How come you're so anxious to get the bulls grinded down if he's still so great?" growled Solórzano, but he didn't say it aggressively; he sounded respectful of the little fat man. "Because he hasn't fought for six months and his eggs are up in his throat with fear. And he's on the big bottle. And I hear he was way off in Mexico last year in spite of the newspapers."

Chaves blew out a sigh, and the chair creaked as he sagged back in it. "Yes, he's stale. And sure, all right, his timing is off, way off. You can't go the way he's been going for ten years and expect anything else. Every other fighter in the world can fight one good fight and then coast through three or four. But Pacote is Pacote, and he's had to fight every fight of his life as though it was the Prensa or the Policía in Madrid. And why do you think they've put him on this pedestal, eh? Why, eh?"

"People always want to see The Best. They'll always want to see the one who gets paid the most."

"No, man, no. It's more than that. Much more than that. It's not just that he's a better bullfighter than any of them! Supposing this Tano Ruiz were better than Pacote. They'd go see him and cheer him, sure, but don't you see, Pacote is more than just the best bullfighter. Each time he goes out in the ring, whether here or Mexico or Peru, everyone says, look, there's a real Spaniard, that's the kind of guts Spaniards used to have when Spain was the Number One nation. That's partly why today is going to be so awful. Because he gets at least double what most fighters get, they expect to see double. And that's impossible. It doesn't work that way. He gets double or triple but he can only do half again what other fighters do. They keep demanding more and more every fight and he hasn't any more to give. He's just a man, after all, and there's just so much a man can do with a bull without eating it alive. He's no magician. The people created a myth around him, which is fine. Fine for the wallet. But the myth has gotten bigger than the man. And the man is smaller than he was."

"He doesn't have to drink and make it worse. Nobody makes him drink the way I hear he's been doing."

"*She* makes him drink. That — that *gachí* does it. She's dragged poor Pacote through the street of bitterness with her tricks. Right through the street of bitterness. He's got more horns than a freight car full of snails. Thank God she's in Granada this month and not messing things up around here." He put his voice into falsetto. "Taking the baths, my dear" — his voice dropped — "while Paco's facing Armageddon." He belched. "He should have been out on the ranches all this time sharpening himself up with the calves. But she doesn't like ranches, so he's either been messing around with her and that crowd or toreando the bottle because he's not with her."

"He should have quit a year ago."

"We said we were going to quit when we got back from Mexico. It was her and that damned Tano Ruiz that did it."

"Y amor propio," said Solórzano. "And self-love."

"And that too," sighed Chaves. "You can't be a great anything without that. That's what makes toreros and that's what kills them. Don't go — I want to talk. I've got to talk — I'm sorry, man, about that — a moment ago, you know. But well, you know, this is a bad day. It's a terrible day for me. I made this boy. You got to help me."

"That's all right," said Solórzano. "I'm nervous, too. More nervous than the sea. I just don't like Miuras, that's all."

"I made him," continued Chaves as though he hadn't heard the apology. "And I love the man. I turned him from a clown to Number One in the world. You should have seen him when I found him. You should have seen the dip in his knees when he did a verónica. It was in Málaga when I happened to see him." Solórzano had heard the story a thousand times. Everyone in Spain knew the story. "It was a nocturnal, and all the kids were bad, but he was the worst. He looked like a stork. All legs and neck. He looked like an undriven nail, one of the newspapers said. And then that face. He took it all so seriously they used to say his face was as dreary as a third-class funeral on a rainy day. The people were dying laughing. They didn't see he was doing all the wrong passes for his build. They didn't see the guts he had to go back and back to the insults and the cushions. But I saw it. I saw this kid had everything I never had. The self-love, the drive, the *having* to be good. I guess if you want to analyze it, it was because of his sister — you know, her being a whore and his family's poverty and all that business. But you knew that, didn't you? How he found her in a whorehouse when he was about fifteen? Just went into a whorehouse one night and there was his sister. Everyone knows it. That's the awful part of it — everyone knows it. If I'd had what that kid had I could have been the greatest bullfighter who ever lived. I had the build — you'd never believe it now — but I did. You don't believe me? I did, I tell you I had the build. And I had a feeling for bulls that even Paco hasn't got, though I didn't have Paco's fighting heart. But I saw I could teach this boy. With my brains and his blood, I saw the sky was the limit, that we could revolutionize bullfighting. And he's the best that ever was or will be. He is Paco. He's me. He's *us* — me and him."

"I'll be moving along now, Pepe."

Chaves went on dreamily as though to himself, his voice husky with emotion. "I jerked him out of those nocturnals and I took him up to the ranch. I fed him up and then I could see he had a perfect build. He had good shoulders and a good butt. You can tell a lot about a man by his butt. He just didn't know how to carry himself, how to walk. The first thing I did was tape splints on his knees. Wouldn't let him in the practice ring without them for three months. That took care of that dip in the knee all right." He gave his breathy, panting laugh at the remembrance. "He still walks stiff-legged in the ring because of that."

"Sure, but I've got to go now."

"Wouldn't let him do any passes but the five classic ones. Then we added the pacotina, of course. That was just an old pass of La Serna's that we frilled up. But only those . . ."

"Listen, Pepe, I got to go now."

"Oh, all right, man. Now we're squared away, aren't we? You'll cut the cattle down?"

"Osú, Pepe, I want to look — "

"You can look good on another fight," Chaves said harshly. "Don't you see he could get killed today! If he coasts all the way and stabs them in the lungs, we'll all be at the dinner tonight having a fine time and getting good and drunk. But Tano is out to commit suicide today to try to show the maestro up. He's out to cut tails and hoofs. Let him. But if Paco starts trying to compete with that kid, he'll be in trouble. If he gets a good bull he'll be inclined to work closer. So that's where you come in. You see to it that every bull arrives at the muleta like lead. They can't blame Paco for not doing anything with an animal that's too shot to charge."

"So I get credit for his flop. I'll need some extra money for that."

"You're already getting plenty! Twice what Tano's men are getting."

"What's the great Pacote worth these days? Forty million pesetas? Fifty? More? He won't miss an extra thousand duros."

"Sure, only five thousand pesetas. And do you think you or I would have the guts to make even one thousand pesetas the way he made those millions? Every peseta stinks of blood, his blood and bull's blood. Sure, he's rich, he'll be the richest man in the graveyard if you don't do what I'm paying you for! All right, we'll make it five more." There was a tearing sound. "Here's half of it." He added significantly: "You get the other half after the fight."

There was a scraping of a chair. Pacote moved quickly

down the hall as he heard Solórzano whine: "Always the hard way, eh Pepe? I'll have to paste them together afterwards. Well, I guess I'll grab me some rest and . . ."

Pacote ducked into his room. He closed the door and leaned back against it and closed his eyes. He could feel the sweat damp on his forehead and prickly on his scalp under his hair.

"Mother of God, Mother of God," he breathed. "Even Pepe, even old Pepe." After a while he opened his eyes. There was a fly on the ceiling. It didn't move — just clung there upside down.

He went to the dresser and took a long drink from the bottle in the drawer behind his socks. He had been partly hiding it from Chaves and partly from himself. He went over to the bed and flopped down on it. He pushed his face that was dark yet pale into the mattress. It smelled soggy and old and a little like blood. He was thinking it would be nice to get the bottle and finish it and at the same time trying to make himself forget this insane idea, when a little knock came on the door. People. Good. The sooner people came the sooner one got into the part and the easier it was to play this rotten game of bullfighter.

"Come in."

She opened the door and stuck her head in impishly, saying in a put-on childish voice: "Is this the room of the famous Pacote and may I please . . ."

"Soco!"

". . . have his autograph, please, please, please?"

7

HE JUMPED UP. He went to her and put his arms around her and kissed her, aiming for her mouth but hitting mostly cheek. The expensive perfume and the faint, good, animal smell of her stung his nostrils like cognac in a snifter glass.

"Ay, Señor Matador," she said, dropping her voice. "Easy on my make-up." She pulled away slightly and wrinkled her nose exaggeratedly. "Drinking?" she chided, "drinking on the day of a fight, Pacotito?"

"That's just from last night," he murmured. "What are you doing down here? I thought you were up there till next week."

"Oh, we just all got the idea to come down for the fight today, so down we came in my little old Citroën. How are the bulls?" She asked it with the same solicitous lack of concern of a person's inquiring after another's head cold, but the fact that she had asked at all pleased him inordinately.

"They're all right. They're fine."

"That's good. That's wonderful, darling. You know, we've got to do something about that streak of yours. It seems even lighter. It's almost white now. Maybe we ought to dye it."

She tugged at the shade and let it roll further up. "Mind?" The sun streamed around her, making her chic white dress from Paris look yellowy white, like the lace in a Velásquez portrait. Her dark brown hair, bobbed attractively out of fashion, was suddenly gilded. The glare gave her wrinkles — wrinkles she didn't really have — around the incredible green eyes. "Sevilla la maravilla," she said mock-poetically. The squinting made her look

slightly Oriental. "Look at Sevilla, now. So sleepy. People home after mass. Taking siestas, eating. Think how gay it will be in a little while."

Oh yes, he thought. Gay as all hell. "How was Granada?"

"Granada?" She watched a carriage clop along around

the tree-lined square and pull up beside the other hacks that nudged the battered taxis, waiting for the big scramble to begin. "Oh, Granada was Granada. Sad. But there were some people there who were very gay. There was this man Ali Ben Mascarenhas, you know, who bought Franco's yacht. He invited us to catch them in Valencia next week and cruise around Morocco. He has a castle in Tangier. He's lots of fun. You'd love him. And the Marqués de La Huerta and Cucú and Norberto and all of them. You know."

He knew. All those people who were so dreadfully gay and rich and well dressed and always asking him questions about bullfighting. And it was lucky they did for they would tune him out, not meaning to, when they discussed other subjects. They didn't at first because they were so impressed by being with the great Pacote. But when they got used to him and found that out of the ring he was just a man, a quiet, shy man who had no small talk and whose entire raison d'être was predicated on the fact that he happened to be able to do one thing better than anyone else in the world, they lost interest. And even about bullfighting they generally spent most of the time telling him *their* ideas on it, which was just as well for Pacote, as he didn't like to talk much anyway, and it was especially boring to talk about the bulls with people who knew just enough about the subject to be able to back up their misconceptions with technical talk. His greatest bond with them was that they all drank too much, didn't work, and had plenty of money. But he didn't even drink the way they did. He drank for oblivion, like a peasant; they went along, never getting falling-down drunk but always in a gentleman's sherry haze. Yet they were probably his best friends. He'd outgrown the few friends of his youth. They were shopkeepers, bartenders, hod carriers, bricklayers now. And it was hard to be good friends with other bullfighters because of rivalry and egotism. No, outside of Pepe, who wasn't accepted by them, these wasters were technically his best friends. And if it were not for Socorro and if it were not for the fact that he was a successful bullfighter, the most successful bullfighter, he would not be their friend. He would be nothing. He would simply be what everyone knew he was — the brother of a whore and the son of a man who died in the poorhouse. Suddenly he realized Socorro had been talking.

" . . . and then when Norberto arrived we did the cutest thing. They hadn't seen each other for a month — since Madrid — and he didn't even know that Cucú was in Andalucía. He thought she was still in San Sebastián! Well! When we arrived at the door of the Duquesa's party, we handed him a ribbon and told him that everyone was to receive a present, and he was to follow it to find out what *his* was. So he began following the ribbon and it went upstairs and down and out into the garden and back upstairs to a closet, and in the closet was Cucú!" She started to laugh. Then louder, and soon she was laughing, not at what had struck her funny but at herself laughing. "Don't you think that was cute? That was my idea. Très amusant, no? Don't you think it was a good one?"

"Very good." Almost good enough to drive away for a moment the blackness of the Miura images that sulked at the edges of his brain.

"They became engaged that night." She always wore the suggestion of a smile that made strangers on the street think they knew her. She looked as though she had hundreds of delicious secrets that she could share if she only wished to. Despite her past — and her present — there was something girlish and fresh and virginal about her. It was as though her exterior had been fashioned with no thought toward who the occupant would be. Even her good figure, untrammeled by constricting undergarments, looked as though it had traces of baby fat.

God, she looked so beautiful. "Why don't *we* become engaged tonight?" He said it lightly, but he almost meant it. Almost meant it in spite of the fact that he knew it could never work.

"Don't you think it would look a little silly on us, darling? Theoretically we've been engaged three years." It was closer to two, but it gave a domestic, warm feeling to stretch it. As she spoke, her green eyes appraised herself in the glass above the bureau; she was a mirror watcher.

"It would please the American Ambassador."

This made her smile automatically at her reflection, for it was an old joke with them. Now they remembered the times they had relived it better than the incident itself. Two years before, he had been lured to Peru, for the first time, for six fights at twenty thousand dollars apiece. The Peruvians took their bullfighting almost as seriously as the Mexicans, and he was lionized beyond belief. They told everyone that they were married; Lima being such a small town socially, it made it easier for everyone. Most people knew better, however, and a delectable subject for Limeños at cocktail parties was whether or not they were married.

In a bid for Peruvian popularity the American Ambassador decided to give a large reception for the visiting matador. Socorro and Pacote were driven to the Embassy by General Graña and his wife, and Pacote happened to escort the General's wife into the large ballroom. The little Ambassador bustled up to them and said in his midwestern twang: "Buenos noches, Mr. and Mrs. P'coty, buenos noches."

"I'm sorry," said Señora Graña, "but I am not Mrs. Pacote."

"Perfectly all right, perfectly all right," the Ambassador said knowingly. "We Americans are broad-minded people."

"But I am *not* Mrs. Pacote!" she insisted.

"Tut tut, my dear," said the Ambassador, "you know that you two are as welcome here as if you *were* married." He then led them into the receiving line and introduced them to the visiting dignitaries. Señora Graña, who had a sense of humor, decided to link her arm in Pacote's and enjoy being the wife of the world's Number One matador. When her husband trailed after her, protesting: "Darling, what the devil is this?", she turned to the Ambassador and said with an airy wave of her hand: "Pay no attention to that man — he's just my husband's sword boy!"

Yes, they had laughed over it so many times that now it was impossible to garner any reaction from it, or even to be positive that it had happened at all.

"We should get married really for the dear little foolish Ambassador," Socorro said brightly. She went to the bureau, opened a drawer, and took out a handkerchief.

"They've mixed in a lot of mine with yours," she said, as she removed a smudge of lipstick from the corner of her full mouth. "So *that's* why I don't have any!" She put several handkerchiefs in her little jeweled purse.

Compadre raised his head, and, looking at Socorro, he gave a familiar half-bark as a sort of afterthought and dropped his head again. Pacote gave him a reassuring pat. Then he noticed her earrings, small and star-shaped and terribly expensive looking. He tried to be casual as he asked: "Those are — those are new, aren't they?"

"Oh, these?" She turned her head sharply, as though if she were quick enough she might get a glimpse of them on her lobes. "They are nice, aren't they?" She frowned. "You know, you ought to get rid of that dog. He smells."

"Granada?" he asked feeling the tightening in his chest.

"It's as though something crawled into him and died." She took a cigarette and match off his bureau and plunked down in the big chair. "Yes, Granada, as a matter of fact" — she nicked the match with a lacquered thumbnail — "and darling, I overdrew at the bank to" — she lit the cigarette and puffed twice — "to pay for them. Do you suppose you could" — she blew out a cloud of smoke — "do something about it?"

She had never bought herself any jewelry in her life — never had had to. The large Brazilian stone on her right hand and the diamond wrist watch, he had given her. Also the little gold bracelet with the brands of the different bull ranches on it, but he never inquired about the origin of the countless other bracelets that clanged on her forearms or the very expensive-looking diamond fish with a ruby

eye that was clipped on the front of her dress. "I'll have
Chaves take care of it in the morning."

It was probably Ali Ben whatever his name was. But it
wasn't true that he had horns, the way Chaves said. Men
were mad for her and any girl liked men's attentions and
that was all there was to it. He knew that before he had
met her she had lived with the man who had directed her
first and only moving picture — a very bad picture. But
she had been faithful to him until he went to England.
And afterwards there was Guilbert, the French sportsman-
racer. He was also sure she had been true to him until his
Alfa-Romeo had gone over an embankment and crushed
the life out of him. And she was true now, in spite of
Chaves, who only said what he said because he hated her.
And then, unaccountably he remembered the refrain Pepe
was fond of quoting: "She's not a whore, she who lies abed
making love with him and them and thee and me — A
whore is she who has the soul of a whore, even though a
virgin she still may be."

"How were the baths?" he asked.

She opened her mouth, let the smoke laze out, and ended
by yawning and giving a half-laugh at herself. He had the
idea she had been drinking. Not much. She was too smart
and too vain to ever drink too much.

"Tired?" he asked.

"Well," she said smiling. "I've been up *all* day!"

God, she had such charm when she smiled. They were
so different, he thought: as different as coal and snow.

"Oh, the baths were fine." She reached over to the other

chair and toyed with the tassels that dangled from the epaulet of the gold costume. She was getting restless already. "It fixed my foie up perfectly."

She loved to use French words, especially in bed, and it annoyed him because he knew she had learned every word from Guilbert.

"Now I am all ready to ruin my foie again by eating too much foie and drinking too much champagne." She had a wayward eyebrow that would assert its independence while she talked and gave her a roguish look. "I have a wonderful idea! Let's take a long walk in the Parque María Luisa right now."

He froze. He stared at her intently as though he hadn't heard her right and his nerves started to take over, almost letting him blurt out: A walk, good Christ, are you mad? But he clenched his hands around the brass end of the bed and compressed his lips flat against his teeth. This aloneness was what killed. This always having to go it alone, no sharing. But he had to control himself. An outburst would just bring on a defensive pout and a mumble of you-never-understand. And it was foolish and childish to say, Why don't you think about me once in a while? So he smiled and forced some warmth into his voice.

"A walk, Soco?"

"Yes, wouldn't it be fun? We can come out on the Palmera, because I told Norberto and Cucú that I'd meet them at the Bi-Lindo for a drink before the — "

She turned around and her face registered distress. "Oh, darling, I forgot that you're fighting today!"

Her apology, something so rare, made him feel superior for a few seconds, and hate welled up inside him for all the times she had hurt him with her indifference.

"Paco, love, how could I have been so thoughtless?" She kissed him.

"That's all right," he said brusquely.

His tone wiped the distress mask from her face, and she turned away sullenly.

He capitulated, as he always did, loathing himself. "That's all right," he said, meaning it this time. He pretended, to her and to himself, that she hadn't really forgotten. "It would be relaxing, take my mind off this business." He made a show of looking at his watch. "But we haven't much time. We'll take a long walk tomorrow."

"But I told La Peñaranda that we'd all go out to the finca for lunch."

He nodded numbly. It didn't make any difference, really. Tomorrow was so far away it seemed as though it were another century.

He looked at his watch again, this time to see what time it was. They'd be here in twenty minutes. He could already hear the steady clop of carriages beginning down in the streets. It wasn't the occasional clop of a dray cart or of a wagon with a plodding horse and lead donkey. It was the brisk, relentless, proud clopping of the fancy carriages rolling down the Palmera from the big homes and country estates. He could hear the gay ching-ching-ching of the harness bells.

"That's twice," said Socorro. She reached way over

and turned on the radio. "You must be nervous. You've looked at your watch twice."

"I'm scared. I'm always scared."

"You're scared? I never knew that."

He thought of saying: I guess there are things you don't know about me. But he said: "My knees start to shake when I see my name on the first contracts. They don't stop until the end of the season. Thank God this is the last."

Conchita Piquer came on the radio in the middle of "Child of Fire." Socorro sang along with her, snapping her fingers in rhythm and writhing a little in the chair: *"Inside my soul I have a fountain, in case your guilt should wish to drink. . . ."* It was gypsy wailing — the "deep singing" of the bronzed folk.

He sat down on the arm of her chair, and as she shook her shoulders and clapped out the time, he could see down the front of her dress. He could see the good breasts that seemed to start their soft swell almost from the collarbone. It was as though he had never seen her undressed. He hadn't had her for weeks now. It was like a glass of water when parched — before having it, there was nothing one wanted more, and after having it there was nothing one wanted less. But he wanted her now.

"Soco . . ."

He slid his hand down the front of her dress and cupped one of her wonderful breasts, gently, letting it sit in his palm. He could see the pink nipple, like the eraser on a pencil, and he could feel it burgeon, feel it swell. He moved his fingers up and pushed the shoulder strap of her dress.

It slipped down to her elbow. The skin was very white compared with the rest of her tanned body, showing the line where she had protected it while sun bathing.

"Ay, Pacorro," Soco murmured, dropping her head over against his chest, watching interestedly in the big mirror as his hand took her breast again. "Such a long time."

"Now, now, *now!*" he whispered in her ear, and her breath quickened automatically. She was easily aroused, always quicker than he, and it was fun to pull this trick on her, even at a crowded cocktail party.

"Vámonos," he breathed, standing up and pulling her to her feet. "Let's go."

"Yes," she said eagerly. She ground her cigarette out in the ash tray. She stepped out of her shoes. Then she crossed her arms, and grasping the hem of her white dress she stripped it off over her head. She had nothing on underneath, but the white where her bathing shorts had been looked like panties against her tan. He put his arms around her feeling her nakedness against him. He felt suddenly terribly in love with her, terribly close to her. After all, this was all they really had in common.

"My love . . ." she said. She pulled away and pranced to the rumpled bed, her breasts bobbing saucily. She sat down on it, crossed her legs primly, cocked her head, and smiled at him mockingly, challengingly.

He shed his dressing gown and walked to the other side of the bed and sat down. When he pulled her down on her back, she squirmed her legs onto the bed ecstatically.

"Darling," she murmured happily as she kissed the scar

on his chest. "Such a very naughty business before a fight, such little bad things . . . "

The fight!

Good God, he'd been able to forget it for a few moments, but now he felt the cold grab down there low in his body, felt his passion ooze into nothingness, felt his masculinity melt away.

"I'd — I'd — " he began. He sat up on the edge of the bed again. Forgotten. Forgotten that even Pepe thought there was a good chance of his getting killed today.

"I was just joking," she said. "Come on, darling." She tried to pull him down on the bed again.

"Paco!"

He stood up abruptly and walked to where he had dropped his dressing gown. After he had put it on he turned around.

"You mean you've got me like this and you're going to leave me?" she exclaimed.

"I'm sorry, Socorro."

"It was your idea," she propped herself up on one arm, "and now you're going to leave me like this?"

"I'm sorry," he said guiltily. "Afterwards. But now — now I'd better save myself for the bulls."

She knew it wasn't that. She knew it was just because he wasn't able to. "Well, this is the first time this has happened," she said, flopping back on the bed.

"Socorro, I . . . "

He came back and lay on the bed beside her, but she rolled away from him, giving him her back. When he started to run his hand over her body, she pulled away and got up. She put on her dress and shoes. Then she turned the radio up louder.

"Don't be angry," he said, getting off the bed. "Can't you understand that I . . ."

"Who's angry?" she said with an indifferent laugh. "I'm not angry. I understand how it is on a day like today."

"You know I love you very much."

She lit a cigarette; then she said: "And I love you, too."

He snapped the radio off.

"Listen," he said, and it came out now by itself, with no pre-thought. "Listen, why don't we get married?"

She looked at him with a half-smile. "How sweet of you, Paquito. If you had asked me two years ago, you never can tell, I might have jumped at the chance." She turned the radio on again, and said "Sa-sa-sa-saa," encouraging the singer.

"I didn't feel it was the life for a woman," he mumbled. What he almost admitted to himself was that he hadn't because he didn't want to marry a woman, no matter how much he loved her, that he wasn't sure he could trust. Not knowing whether she loved him or just the Pacote legend and aura and money.

But God, how he loved her, and now he felt an urgency, that he must marry her, or she would slip from him forever, that everything would slip from him. *That everything would slip from him!*

"No life for a woman?" she exclaimed. "It's a wonderful life for this woman. I like it. I like the excitement.

I like the people. I like the traveling. I like the crowds."

"And now?"

She shook her head. "You say this is your last fight. Then what? Sit on a ranch in back of Córdoba and watch the bulls and weeds grow? Not for me, Paco darling. I came from the country, the poor country, the dirty country, the drab country; I don't ever want to go back. I like the sparkle of the city and the sparkle of the people you meet in the city. I might even make another moving picture. I'm only twenty-seven. I'm on top and heading up."

The way she said it was almost as though she'd added: And your star is beginning to fizzle, my friend.

"Don't you ever want to be normal and have a home and children?" he asked. "Live quietly? Get to know yourself?"

She looked at him bemused, and her eyebrow went up.

"You *must* be scared, Paco. I've never heard you talk so much or so fancy. I want a drink. And hand me my purse, will you?"

He took out the bottle from behind his socks.

"Ah," she said "a bureau-drawer drinker."

He felt himself flush a little as he poured a drink for her. "Say when."

"Epá," she said when the glass was a fifth full.

He wanted one himself. God, how he wanted one, but he could already feel the others too much.

"In the first place, chico," she said, taking a drink, and making a face at the glass, "as long as we're being so dreadfully frank, we're not normal, thee and me. People who become actresses and bullfighters aren't normal. You take your choice, the glitter and the gold or the farm and the kids. You can't have them both." She took a comb from her purse and ran it through her hair repeatedly, talking with her head tilted way over. "And I wonder if you really do want the farm and the kids. At one time in your life you might have. But while you were trying to get where you could retire to the good life, you made yourself into somebody who never could stand the good life. Because you aren't anybody or anything but Pacote now. Stop me if I'm talking too much, but I just came from a big luncheon, and the wine was flowing." She laughed for no reason and drank again. "You stop being the great Pacote and you stop being. You just don't exist. And I don't think you'd like not existing, chico, any more than I would. Don't think I'm being too harsh, Paco. Just frank."

She waggled her empty glass, and he took it from her and poured another drink.

"So you," he tried to control his voice, "you won't come to Córdoba with me?" In a way, he wanted her to say it, as if in the saying of it would be a contract that she would leave him, that he would be free of her forever. It would end the confusion, the indecision, the agony, and yet, of course, he knew that he could never want to be free of her.

"Oh, that's a long way off," she said. Only it came out, "Hat's a-hong hay aw," because now she was looking into her compact mirror and applying lipstick.

"I'll be going up there next week," he said significantly.

"That's very soon." He saw her drink sitting there on the arm of the chair, golden and wonderful in the sun, and he wanted to snatch it up and gulp it down.

"No, let's go to Morocco next week. The whole gang is going on Franco's yacht." Defiantly, she snapped her compact shut and looked up at him. "Don't you think it would be très chic to go on the Generalísimo's yacht?"

"Chaves and I are going to set up the ranch next week," he said sternly, and there was an ultimatum in his tone.

"Well, you can damn well go alone," Socorro said, suddenly sulky. "And see how you like sleeping with Chaves." She turned the radio up louder, castanetting her fingers irritatedly with the music and humming along: "*Tell me, woman, if you can, when a love dies — where does it go?*"

He reached over and snapped the radio off.

"You mean — this is the end of us?"

"I mean I'm not going to rot on a ranch in Córdoba or any other place." She turned the radio on again. "And I'm not going to play brood mare to your stallion!"

"And if I weren't getting out of the game?"

"Well, I guess we'd just go on the way we are. Oh, darling, I don't see what you're quitting for anyway. You're on top, you're still young. Twenty-nine's not old. Take Ortega — he's almost forty-five. It's that salamander Chaves who's talked you into it."

"Look!" He ran his fingers through the gray streak in his hair exasperatedly. "Look, now look — I should have quit a year ago, and Pepe had nothing to do with it, and all this isn't helping my nerves much."

"Well, don't get so excited," she said soothingly.

"Maybe if you didn't drink so much, you wouldn't be so jumpy."

He laughed, something he did only when he did not think something was funny. Then he said slowly: "There are two black animals over in the stalls right now just quivering there in the dark waiting to kill me in" — he shoved back the sleeve of his dressing gown and looked at his watch — "in an hour, and you tell me not to be jumpy."

"Caray, Paco," she complained, "you were never like this before."

"I — I was me before," he said. He went to the bureau abruptly. He poured four inches of whiskey into a glass and drank most of it at one gulp. He felt its heat sock his stomach and the good warm numbing up the back of his neck. He filled the glass up again.

"Darling, you need a rest, your nerves are all shot." It was the tone that did it. She said it clinically. She said it coldly, from a long way away.

"You're in a hell of a state. Why don't you come down on Ali Ben's yacht with us? We're going to have a wonderful time, and in a month or two you can start fighting again and be the old Pac — "

He whirled and shot the whisky in her face. It wasn't a very big glass, but she gasped as if a cold ocean wave had broken over her. She jumped up, trembling, her breath coming hard.

"Now you've done it, you damned peasant!" she snarled. She swallowed twice as she tried to organize the torrent of emotions suddenly set to seething inside her. The whiskey, was dripping down her face and running down the front of her dress. "And you had the nerve to ask me to marry you! You were perfectly happy to keep me just your mistress for years because you didn't think I was good enough to marry. Now that you're through you come begging me to marry you. Me marry a eunuch? Me marry the shell of a man? Me marry somebody who's so shot he has to drink his guts out of a bottle? The great Pacote!" She spat out a laugh. "The great Pacote who just wants to crawl off to Córdoba and rot on a farm like the peasant he is. I don't know why I've stuck with you and your nerves this long. The great Pacote! The great ball-less wonder! And of course your nerves are gone! You know this kid is going to show you up today — you know you've got to quit before you get killed, and you know that when you quit you'll be nothing, and you can't face it! You can't face being just a picknose peasant and . . ."

"And the brother of a whore," he cut in quietly. "I thought you'd get around to that. Yes, sure. The brother of a whore, and the lover of a whore. You'd better go if you're going to have a drink with your friend before the corrida."

She strode to the door. "I hope they make a sieve out of you today," she said, through her teeth.

Then she was gone, and he wasn't quite sure why things had happened as they did, but in a way he felt good about it, the decision was over. And in another way he wanted a drink very badly. He had it. As he threw it down he noticed that the fly was still clinging to the ceiling and hadn't moved. He poured another drink. Drinking had got him into this mess, and now, he thought foolishly, it could get him out. Drink enough and the bulls would go away, everybody'd go away. There'd be no corrida.

8

HE HAD BEEN semi-drunk when he had agreed to this fight. What else was there for a retired matador to do in the city? You either drank or you sat around regaling worshipers with tales of ring triumphs — and Pacote didn't like bull talk about himself.

That day he and Socorro were at Chicote's, rendezvous of the pigtailed folk in Madrid. Young Tano Ruiz had come in with his two brothers. They had sent over a bottle of champagne, and Pacote had to reciprocate by inviting them to his table. Tano hoped he would have "the honor of performing on the same bill with the maestro," and Pacote reminded him that he was retired. Then it was clever the way they did it. Somehow they rigged the conversation so that soon one brother was on his feet announcing to the whole restaurant that Pacote was retiring because he was scared to appear in the same ring with Tano and that Pacote was afraid of Miuras. This last charge was not completely unfounded, for "the bulls of death" had killed seven famous matadors, including his uncle; Pacote remem-

85

bered as a child his uncle dying in their house after three months with drains in his hip; he remembered the stench and the screaming. Once during the bloody century of Miura breeding, all the bullfighters had banded together and formed a pact never to accept animals from that stable. Pacote had only fought them once and had done badly. But here in the café, although he had tried to control himself, knowing that the Ruiz brothers were just trying to goad him into a lucrative and prestige-making fight, all he knew was that he was being insulted in front of Socorro and all the people in the restaurant and that he was a better and more honest torero than this young punk would ever be. He did what they wanted him to do, played right into their hands. He stood up and accepted the challenge. Chaves would have stopped him, but Chaves wasn't there. When he found out, it was too late, for the newspapers had it — the Ruiz clan had seen to that.

So now Pacote drank and poured another. He lurched across the room, putting the bottle on the bedside table, and flopped down on the bed, his eyes tightly closed, his head buried in the pillow, his whole body shuddering. The dog came over and licked his face, and Pacote pushed it away. He opened one eye and saw a spot on the bed, a brown burn spot. He whirled and looked up at the ceiling and that damned fly was still there.

"Fly?" he said, his voice going up at the end. Then "Fly!" with his voice going down on the end. Then: "Fly-fly," very quickly. He gave a groan-laugh.

Lola Flores was giving the final bleats of her song: *"Tell me, woman, when a love dies, where does it go?"*

Pacote drew back his fist and shot it into the radio. His hand smashed through the lattice work and cloth of the speaker and the music stopped, but the light was still on and it hummed. He swept it off the table and it crashed to the floor.

He wanted to shout. He did shout, muffling it in the pillow. Then he took the pillow and flung it at the fly on the ceiling. He didn't hit it, but the draft dislodged the fly, and it spiraled down, a dry shell. It had been dead for some time.

"That's me," he said. He gave one laugh. "Dead as a hammer and clinging, clinging, clinging, cling . . ."

Through the fog he heard a knock on the door. "A moment!" he mumbled. His thoughts were swirling in strange, slow patterns, like cream when it's poured in iced coffee, but he wasn't quite over the brink. He lay on his back and tilted the bottle straight up, holding it there in his mouth, his tongue controlling the flow of the liquid, the bottle gurgling happily, his Adam's apple bobbing. When it was empty he gasped: "All right!"

Chaves came in. "Well, she gone? We've only got about an hour. Got to do a fast job of . . ."

Pacote propped himself up on his elbows. "Hola, Pepe," he said foolishly. "Pepe, what d'ya think?" The words tumbled over one another in slow motion. "I'm a fly on the wall and I'm dead and I'm clinging just the same."

Chaves groped behind him for a chair and sagged slowly into it.

Pacote winked as though imparting a fine secret. "Dead as a hammer," he whispered confidentially, "but hanging on, hanging on."

Chaves could only stare in fascinated horror. "Oh God," he breathed, "oh God."

"Y'know," Pacote said mournfully, "we're all out of another age. That's what the American said. El Pimpi is a centaur, and I'm the god of the dance. Never knew that, did you? And Pepe Chaves is a wood sprite who hides in dark places at the base of a tree and looks out with eyes as big as a toad's. Looks out to see if he can find a little gangrene for his dinner. And that's not fair, all the gangrene in the forest belongs to me, me, old Paco Gangrene, the god of the dance."

Pepe mopped his brow and wiped his fat neck with the wig. "That bitch," he said. "Oh, that crab-laden bitch." Then he sprang into action. He barked orders into the telephone for coffee and food. He went into the bathroom and ran the cold water in the bath.

"Get up, you bastard." He helped Pacote up from the bed. He put his arm around him and started him for the bathroom. "Walk, now."

"Don't want to walk," Pacote mumbled.

"Walk!" Pepe commanded, and Pacote started his legs going.

"Amigo de mi arma," Pacote said, patting Chaves's fat stomach. "Friend of my soul, you fight today. The Miuras will give you the old high colonic 'stead of me."

"That bitch," Pepe said. "Oh, that bitch."

Pacote tenderly stroked the bald head as he walked. "Don José Chaves, father of ten and hero of the battle of Trafalgar. Olé for Don José Chaves."

In the bathroom, Chaves stripped the dressing gown off him.

"Get in," he said, pushing Pacote down to a sitting position on the edge of the bathtub.

"José Chaves, my friend, your friend, defender of the weak, righter of wrongs . . ."

"Get in," commanded Chaves.

" . . . hater of lies, enemy of castration, deflowerer of . . ."

"Get in!"

" . . . deflowerer of adolescents and small rodents." Pacote got in the tub and gasped at its shock. He lay in it limply. "How does it go, Pepe?" he mourned. "A man's love for a woman waxes and wanes like the moon, but — but a man's love for his brother, how does it go, Pepe?"

Chaves put his hand on top of Pacote's head and shoved him under. "Is as steadfast as the stars," he said mechanically, holding him there.

He let him up spluttering and gagging when he heard the knock on the door. It was the waiter.

"No way to treat the god of the dance," Pacote muttered reproachfully, as Chaves brought the tray into the bathroom and put it on the stool. Flipping the lid down on the toilet, Chaves sat down. He started to reach over toward the tub, but Pacote saw it coming and obediently slid under the water holding his nose. When he came up, Chaves shoved a large cup of coffee at him.

"Nectar for the god of the dance," Chaves growled. "Drink!"

Pacote took the cup shakily. "Pepe, I've been to Biarritz, you know."

"Yes, sure, you're a gardenia," said Chaves. "A regular gardenia. Drink!"

Between immersions, Chaves fed him the small pot of

coffee and the steak. And then he fed him another pot, Pacote coughing, protesting, spewing some of it up. In twenty minutes he was able to get out of the tub, dry himself, and make it into the other room under his own power. He was still drunk, but he was sober enough to realize that he was drunk and to be afraid because of it.

The telephone rang, and the concierge said that the newspapermen wanted to come up. Chaves snapped, "Not yet," and hung up.

He handed Pacote the white cotton underwear, and he got into it. It came to his knees and elbows. There was a knock on the door.

"Good day, señores." The barber came in timidly, putting each foot down as though apologizing to the carpet for stepping on it. He was a little sparrow of a man who bowed several times and otherwise gave evidence of his pleasure at being the honored one selected to shave the great Pacote before his last fight. Pacote sat down, and the barber readied his instruments. He sloshed up a lather and began to shave him, but he had trouble accomplishing his mission because Pacote's head kept lolling. When he left, Chaves sighed.

"Well, let's call it off," he said quietly, "It never should have been anyway."

"Like hell," said Pacote.

"We'll just say you're sick."

"Like hell. I'm all right." He started to fumble on the long white stockings. Suárez, the swordhandler, stuck his monkey head in the door.

"It's about time!" exclaimed Chaves.

"U'té' perdone," said Suárez, with a one-finger conciliatory salute. He crossed the room very businesslike and dropped to his knees in front of Pacote. He skillfully pulled on the cotton stockings, smoothing them up the long, slightly bowed legs. Then the rose stockings went over them. Pacote stood up and took up the white silk pants heavy with the crusted gold designs. He swayed and almost fell as he tried to balance to get one leg into the pants.

"Mata'or," said the wizened little man, his eyes pinched with fear. "You're not going to fight like this?"

"Like what, you whoreson?" He had never spoken roughly to a menial before in his life. "Shut up and get me into this filthy taleguilla."

The little man swallowed, but he supported Pacote while the other leg was guided into the pants.

"Just say the word, Pacote," said Chaves, "and I'll call Manolo Belmonte and tell him that . . ."

"Shut up and grab."

Chaves took one side of the high pants and Suárez the other. They lifted hard while Pacote writhed and worried his narrow hips so that the crotch of the skin-tight pants was right. Then he sat down on the bed and extended his legs while Chaves and Suárez did up the complicated strings and tassels at the knee — the machos had to be just right, tight without hindering the leg action.

Pacote usually put in his own cuff links and studs to give him something distracting to do. But his hands were shaking too much, so Suárez did it. He had just buttoned the pleated shirt and knotted the thin red tie when the telephone on the wall rang.

Chaves grabbed it. "Diga," he grunted impatiently. "Sí,

diga, sí, sí, sí, al aparato." Then he covered the mouth-
piece and said to Pacote. "I think it's going to be your
señora madre from San Sebastián."

"Good Christ," breathed Pacote.

"Do you want to talk to her?"

"Christ, no."

"Go ahead, San Sebastián," said Chaves into the telephone. Then in the high unctuous tone he reserved for
priests and older women: "Sí, señora, sí! How are you?
Certainly he's all right. He's fine, very calm. No, he's not
here at the moment. He . . ."

Pacote walked over to him unsteadily.

"Just a minute, señora, here he is now."

"Hola, Mamá?" Pacote tried to keep his voice controlled and low. "How is San Sebastián? What? I don't
hear you very well. Oh. Oh. Oh. Well, that's good.
Yes, it's fine here, too. No. No wind, a Dios gracias. No,
I haven't seen the bulls, but I hear they are very little. No,
honestly, Pepe said they are real pollywogs. And horns
like bananas. I sound differently? It's a bad connection."

Suárez was kneeling and sliding Pacote's feet into the
black slippers as he talked.

"Yes, this is the last, I swear it. Now please stop crying,
Mamá, for God's sake, there's nothing to cry about. You
read it in the papers didn't you? This is the last one. And
I'm going to stay a mile away from the cattle. Yes, Pepe
will call you from the plaza, and I'll see you in a week on
the ranch. Stop crying, for God's sake." And then on an
impulse, because he knew it would please her, he added:
"And Mamá — she — she won't be there."

After he had hung up, the image of the good fat woman with the tragic face and the same heavy-lidded eyes as his made him feel like crying for a moment, and he didn't know why. Chaves gave him the red sash. Pacote held one end against his waist and spun slowly into Chaves, who pulled on the other end.

After the sash was on, he sat down, and Suárez clipped the velvet button and artificial pigtail to a lock of hair high on the back of Pacote's head. The pigtail had been made two years ago from Socorro's brown hair for luck, and it looked almost blond against the blue-blackness of Pacote's wet hair.

The telephone rang. Chaves took it angrily, then turned to Pacote. "The concierge says there's a bunch down there who are hollering to come up and watch you dress. Salazar from the A.B.C. and some foreign newspaperman and K-Hito and that American and the Marqués of Aracena and the rest."

"Tell them I'm already dressed and to go hell." He put on the embroidered vest. "Water."

Suárez brought him a glass from the bathroom. It was the one that the whiskey had been in, and the smell made him think he might throw up. But he drank it. Never had he been so dry, fear-dry and whiskey-dry. It was as though he had brushed his teeth with mucilage; it was an actual effort to open his mouth or swallow.

Pepe helped him into the stiff heavy jacket. It was a beautiful thing, the gold designs clustered in simple flower patterns on the white silk. The suit was old now, and here and there was the shadow of a stubborn bloodstain, especially around the waist where the bull's shoulder had brushed by, but it had taken Casa Manfredi three months to make and was the finest they'd ever turned out. Pacote ran his hands down his thighs and the heavy metallic feel of the brocade was good. He felt more like a torero now, more like Pacote than he had in his skinny nakedness half an hour before. Everything he had looked better in the uniform; his wide shoulders, the nonexistent hips and behind and even the saber legs made him a taurine tailor's dream.

Matagatos came in without knocking. He was dressed in his uniform, a cheap version of Pacote's, only blue. "El Buick is in front. How goes it, Pacorro? Not much time."

"Bien, bien," said Pacote. The older man was his cousin and though they weren't exactly close, there was affection and respect there that always made him like himself better. He didn't want Matagatos to see he had been drinking. He turned away and went to the bureau and lit the thick candle in the votive glass. He knew he was swaying a little.

Chaves looked at his watch and jerked his head to the others. "Vámonos ya!"

"A la lucha" announced Matagatos solemnly. "To the battle!"

"Do you always have to say that?" Pacote snarled. Matagatos always said it and Pacote hated the expression.

"Sorry, Pacorro, but let's get going."

Suárez took the tooled leather sword case from the closet, and he and the banderillero went out. Chaves hesitated at the door.

"Paquito," he began hesitantly, "let's call it off, eh? You're in no shape to — "

"Get out of here!" Pacote said.

When Chaves was gone and he was all alone, he dropped his face in his hands. He left them there for a while and then dragged them away, and it felt as though his flesh would pull off from under his fingers.

He could hear the racket in the street — loud now, the cries, the honkings, the vendors, the rattle of carriage wheels over cobbles, the harsh clang of the extra streetcars. He, Pacote Torres, was responsible for all this excitement.

On the dresser in the center was the little gold triptych of the Virgen de la Marcarena, and the candle flickered in front of it. Pacote crossed himself and stood before it simply, devoutly, believing, the palms of his hands together. He had always been embarrassed by any more elaborate procedures.

"Most saintly of Virgins," he said, "I don't ask to be good today. This is not like the other days. I only ask that they come out easy, that they don't snag me, that I may live and be able to worship you. Just let me live. Amen."

He crossed himself again and kissed his thumb which made a cross against his forefinger.

He blew out a long sigh. Picking up the kinky montera off the chair, he held it in both hands by its knobs and dipped his head into it. He pressed it down with the palm of his hand until it came level with his thick eyebrows. He took a handkerchief out of the drawer and put it in the little slit pocket in the side of his jacket.

He patted the dog. And then because it didn't have long to live and had brought him luck for so many years, he held it to him convulsively, hugging it to his chest with tears in his eyes, not really for the dog but for everything.

"Aí, dear Compadre, how you stink."

Then he was as ready as he would ever be. He took the folded dress cape, slung it over his forearm, and left the room. And now it was the time, the real time, the terrible time, the sick-making time, and he felt as brittle and spindly as a lone reed in a monsoon.

9

HE WALKED down the one flight, and the thick carpet felt soft under his slippered feet. He almost stumbled once, but he caught himself and made it the rest of the way down all right. There were little knots of people in the big crowded lobby; and he spotted the flash of color of Matagatos and Cascabel, the other banderillero. They were talking to Chaves and the newspapermen and smoking hard. As he started for them, the crowd saw him and broke into spontaneous applause. It was sincere. Because this was his last and because he'd been great and honest torero. He nodded to them and held himself erect and was careful how he walked; he was still tight physically, though he was thinking almost sober. Some flash bulbs went off, but he couldn't see from where.

People were saying things to him as he pushed through the crowd, but he didn't bother to hear them. The bull critics around Chaves greeted him respectfully, and Pacote reciprocated, but he was thinking: Thank God, I'll never have to sweat about these affable vultures again. And he knew that no matter how much Chaves had paid them they would write the truth today, for it was his last, and they knew that next season there'd be no little envelopes with big bills in them sent over before the fight.

"Historic day today," wheezed Salazar, a great untidy blob of a man. "A great day and a sad day."

"It's the fiesta brava's greatest loss, Maestro," said Camino of the Sevilla "Hoy," rubbing the palm of one hand over the knuckles of the other.

"Es verdad," said the pale foreign correspondent. Pacote knew he was English by his friendly lack of ease and his bad Spanish. "Mucho."

What did one answer to asinine remarks like that?

He felt like saying something startling like: Have you attacked your grandmother again since I last saw you? But he knew anything he said would be drunken talk so he said nothing and turned toward the entrance. Chaves took his arm, and with Matagatos on the other side and Cascabel in front, he was convoyed out of the hotel. He heard murmurs of "Suerte, suerte" from all the people, and he thought: You bastards, you don't want *me* to have luck. You just want *you* to get a thrill out of my risking my neck, want to see me spill my blood.

The big blue station wagon they'd brought back from Mexico was waiting in front, the canvas basket with the folded capes strapped to the grill on top. Suárez, the sword handler, was at the wheel.

Casabel held open the paneled door of the back seat. Pacote edged in, sat down stiffly and cautiously because of the tightness of the costume, and then folded in his long

legs. Chaves climbed in on the other side. Cascabel closed
the door, got in front, and they drove off jerkily; Suárez
hadn't yet mastered the subtleties of "el Buick."

"Great driver, this uncle," Chaves said. "Let's see if you
can get us to the plaza without killing us, eh? I know it's
at least five hundred yards away, but let's just see if you
can make it. Watch those uncles in the street, eh? We
don't mind widowing their women, but let's not dent the
car."

The boulevard, dead an hour ago, was now filled with
mobs of people and taxi-carriages and Italian and French
cars all heading down the wide tree-lined Paseo de Colón
toward the Plaza de Toros Most of the men wore dark
suits, white shirts buttoned at the throat, and no ties. Some
wore black sombreros Cordobeses, the broad brim tipped
over one eye and a toothpick in the band. Mu' flamenco.
Some of the women in the carriages wore mantillas and
snapped their fans open and closed. But there weren't
many of those because it was not fair time. However, there
was more excitement in the air than any regular Feria fight
could produce.

The car was surrounded by people, and some patted the
fenders and rapped on the window and shouted, "Luck,
Luck!"

"A los toros!" men called across the street to each other
jubilantly. "To the bulls!"

The car drove slowly by the open bodegas where the
aficionados were gulping down their café con leche or a
last manzanilla or filling their leather wine bottles. They
would look up when the station wagon went by and yell:

"Olé tu madre!" or "Suerte, Matador!" One held up a bottle and pointed to the label to show he was drinking "Anís Pacote," and Matagatos chuckled. Matagatos wasn't going to risk his neck; he could chuckle.

"Qué tal?" asked Chaves quietly. "How are you going it now?"

Pacote waggled his hand. "Regular, regular."

"Are you still — " Chaves didn't want to embarrass him in front of the two banderilleros — "How do you feel?"

"Better, I guess. Regular."

"I'll get the order switched so you don't fight first."

"I don't want any favors from that uncle."

"It's no favor. He'll be glad to do it."

"I heard what you told Solórzano. About cutting them down. Don't like him, don't like that uncle."

"I'm — I'm sorry you overheard all that manure." Chaves frowned. "It was just a lot of manure I was talking. You're in the best shape of your life."

Pacote snorted air out through his nose in answer.

"I don't like Solórzano either," said Chaves, "but we need him today you know, to — to sort of play safe. He'll cut them down for us. I'm sorry you heard all that stuff."

"Don't like him. He didn't do anything when you pissed on him. Nothing. When you called him a butcher he didn't do anything. When a man gets pissed on I like to see him turn color."

"Like litmus paper," said Chaves. "But I'm sorry you had to hear all that hay."

"Sure, like litmus. But he just took it. Just took it."

"The crowd's going to kill him today for ruining the bulls. He'll turn color when the crowd pisses on him."

"The crowd's going to kill me today. Watch them piss on me today."

"No, they'll blame it on him. You'll be all right. Don't worry about what the crowd thinks. Just get through. Just keep thinking about the ranch and that parlor of yours and the fish in the pond and your mother and about getting drunk tonight. Remember what Belmonte said about the crowd. Keep remembering that."

"Jesús, Jesús," Pacote breathed.

The fear and the whiskey and the motion of the car and the quick stops for the pedestrians was making him sick. His face was wet with sweat and greenish. It would be terrible if he threw up. He had always been so calm before, the one who made everyone else feel there was nothing to fear. He talked to distract himself.

"And how goes the great Cascabel?" he said. "How goes the great Desperdicios?"

Cascabel turned around in the front seat. He grinned, but he was suffering. "Fine, Pacorro, fine."

He was young for a banderillero — Pacote's age — and he was a good kid. He had wanted to be a matador, but he had wanted to be a matador more than he had wanted to do the things a matador must do, and it should be the other way around. He had semi-flopped in his presentation as a novillero in Madrid nine years ago. He hated to kill and disliked the responsibility of being the head man, and, besides, he had no guts with anything but a perfect animal. He could have gone on to be a mediocre matador, perhaps, but he had ideals, and when he saw Pacote fight for the first time, he said, "Here is genius, and I have no business claiming the same title as he has." But he couldn't stay

away from the bulls, and he liked putting in the sticks, so
he joined Pacote's cuadrilla as a banderillero and thought
he was lucky to get with the new "fenómeno." He'd been
with him all this time, through "the alternative" when
he became a senior matador, Mexico and Peru both times,
and now the last.

"There's no wind, anyway," said Pacote. "It's a good
day anyway. Good as bread."

"No," said Cascabel, grinning. "No wind to frig the
cloth."

God, this uncle could grin at anything. If they were
going to hang him, he'd grin because they'd left the price
tag on the rope.

"What are you going to do after today?" Pacote asked.
"What are you going to do with your declining years?"

"I d-don't know." He had a slight speech impediment
that became more pronounced when he was scared. "I
might go with young Juanito Belmonte."

"You can do better than that, Desperdicios." He called
him that affectionately because in the old days there was a
very brave fighter who had the same last name as Cascabel.
Once in a fight the bull's horn had gouged out the man's
eye, and as it was lying on his cheek he had casually reached
up, jerked it all the way off, flicked it away, and gone on
fighting; the people afterwards always called him "Desperdicios" — Cast-off-scrap-of-meat. "I can help you do better than that."

"I d-don't know. Everyone seems to have his cuadrilla
set up."

"You're a great doctor of the barbs. You could go with
Tano Ruiz."

Cascabel made the noise of spitting, though his mouth was too dry to actually produce anything. "I could contract tuberculosis, too."

"Why don't you be smart and quit?"

"I'd sure as hell like to quit right this minute. But after the fight, I won't want to quit. When I s-sit around Los Corales and get drunk, I'll think it's the greatest g-goddamn thing in the world. The day before the fight I always get so scared I call up my brother-in-law and say all right, I'll take that job wholesaling salami right after this last fight, and then after the fight I always call him up, and insult him and tell him to take his job and his s-s-salami and s-s-stuff it. But God, how I'm suffering now. How we suffer, eh, Paco? Why do we do it?"

Pacote held up his hand and rubbed his thumb and forefinger together significantly.

"N-no," said Cascabel. "It must be more than that. It's got to be more than that."

Yes, thought Pacote, it had to be a hell of a lot more than that.

They drove along the Guadalquivir, turned down a narrow street and pushed through the people up a cobbled alley, and then they were in back of the Plaza de Toros. Suárez stopped the car and they got out. Suárez and a mozo waiting there stood on the running board to get the cape basket down. There was a crowd milling around to see the matadors arrive, and Cascabel had to shove a wedge through them up to the great gate.

Chaves beat on the gate with his fat fist. Immediately a little door cut into the larger one opened cautiously and then all the way when the beady eye saw who it was. Pacote tripped on the high sill and almost fell, but Chaves caught him.

"You can't fight this way, chico," he hissed.

"Hell I can't! I'll be all right after the first bull."

The photographers were in the little courtyard, and the No-Do newsreel camera began grinding away. Pacote stopped off at the latrine. When he came out the photographers were heading for the arena and choice positions. Pacote went in to the patio de caballos.

The shaded courtyard was taut and quiet and precisely active compared to the frenetic wantonness of the outside. The four picadors, both Tano's and Pacote's, were near their nags lengthening stirrups, adjusting the peto mattress on the animals' right side, being boosted on. Fat Solórzano was complaining about his mount. The drag mules with their red and yellow plumes were being hitched to the whiffletree. The men in the butchering section were donning white aprons and sharpening knives already. There was the smell of urine and cigar smoke and fear in the air.

Solórzano and the other picador, El Pimpi, nodded unsmilingly to their matador, and Pacote acknowledged it by raising his eyebrows. He followed Chaves toward the big tunnel that led under the stands and under all the people in the cheap sunny section of the ring. Suárez passed them carrying the sword case and the Indian-red water jug and towels around his neck. Behind him trotted the mozo in canvas sandals, running with his knees bent to absorb the weight of the cape basket perched on his left shoulder. Pacote wanted to stop Suárez and get a drink of water — God, he was dry — but it would be too conspicuous; going to the latrine was bad enough. And anyway Suárez was already through the cuadrilla gate and into the ring, going down the alleyway behind the fence to the shady side of the stands. They said old Lagartijo was able to spit copiously before going into the ring to show his contempt for fear, but they were liars.

"You'd better hurry if you're going in there," Chaves said. Tano Ruiz's men were coming out of the door to the little tiled room fitted out like a chapel.

"I'm not going," he said, "it's done." He didn't want to be alone again.

Chaves handed him a lighted cigarette, and Pacote took it gratefully and sucked on it, holding it cupped in his hand as though hiding it. He had just gone to the latrine, but he had to go again. The big fear-leak.

"Buenas tardes," a voice said. "Good afternoon, matador."

Niño de Ronda came out of the chapel.

Pacote had almost forgotten about Niño de Ronda. He was dressed in a wretched purple and black costume that was frayed and stained and had been clumsily let out to accommodate the large bump of stomach. He had his montera in his hand and the bald head glistened. He hadn't even enough fringe in back to clip the añadido to, so he had tied a wide black ribbon around his head and hung the pigtail from that. It looked ridiculous.

"Christ in His pain!" Pacote exploded. He reached out and grabbed the pigtail and jerked it off and flung it on the ground. "Are you out to make me look like a fool?"

Niño de Ronda hung his head like a small boy and mumbled something about being sorry he didn't have any hair to clip a pigtail on to. Pacote snatched the montera out of the man's hands and jammed it on the bald head.

"Take it easy," Chaves warned. "The ribbon won't show with his montera on."

Pacote was quivering, and he needed to drink water and he needed to make water, and it felt as though the skin had been peeled from every nerve in his body. He strode away back up the passageway and around the corner to the latrine. He was afraid he might let go when the trumpet sounded for the bull. Wasn't so bad if you had a dark traje de luces on, but it would be disaster with this white silk. He saw the gate he had come in, and he thought how easy it would be to slip out and run, run anywhere, run to the ranch, run to Mexico where he was treated like a king, run to Peru, run to Buenos Aires where no one knew him, just run, hide.

After relieving himself and adjusting the complexities of the costume, he went back to the cuadrilla gate. Tano Ruiz was there and Chaves was talking to him. Pacote could see his gold and green costume, new and stiff and tight over his woman's behind.

"Hola," said Tano as Pacote came up.

Pacote nodded. He was fighting the urge to yawn, the sign that one is really scared.

"Chaves here wants me to fight first," said Tano in his precise way. "But I just can't see any sense in it." He always held his humorless mouth askew as though shaving or as though he was biting the inside of it. He was tanned and too good looking and as sure of himself as a middleweight champion. He was only twenty, but his father had started him fighting professionally when he was ten as a becerrista — a calf-fighter — and then he was the top novillero for two years before he took the alternative. Two years as a senior matador had given him great command and poise and a hard pair of eyes that belied his unmanly, almost effeminate face.

"But hell, what's your objection?" said Chaves. "We'll be taking the one-twenty. You ought to be glad to get rid of that one-twenty."

"The bulls aren't the point," said Tano. He always frowned as he strove for intense earnestness. "It's just that Pacote is the senior sword and as such he should fight first."

"But this is a mano a mano, and it doesn't matter! He isn't going to have to kill someone else's bull. If it were a regular fight with three matadors it would be different."

Tano shook his head. "I just can't see it."

Chaves's voice was trembling. "Listen, Ruiz, if you want me to beg, I'm begging. Not fighting first is terribly important to us. Paco's not feeling well."

"Yes," Tano grinned. "I can smell his sickness."

"Ruiz, I'm begging you. Let . . ."

"Christ, Pepe," Pacote broke in, "tell the son of a bitch to . . ."

They heard a bolt shoot back, and the cuadrilla gate was suddenly opened, and the sun flashed in where they were standing. It was so bright Pacote couldn't see for a minute. He shook out his dress cape, also white silk with gold leaves and flowers. Draping it over his left shoulder, he gathered the ends around his waist and clutched them with his left hand, the arm resting in the folds like a sling. He stepped forward into the mouth of the gate, and now he could see the dazzling golden sand, finely crushed rock, really, which only the Maestranza plaza had. He could see the whole shady side of the plaza and part of the sunny side, and it was jammed with fifteen thousand people. There it was, the Big Circle, eager to swallow him. He worked his feet back and forth in the sand like a boxer and dropped the cigarette and stepped on it carefully, feeling it under the thin-soled slipper. Matagatos lined up in back of him and then Niño de Ronda, and then Cascabel. And behind he heard the clatter of the four picadors' horses coming down the inclined passageway, skidding a bit on the cobbles. Behind them would be the four mules and the monosabios — the "wise-monkeys" to manage them.

The two "alguaciles" — the constables — pushed their horses down the passageway to the front of the men. They were fancily dressed in black velvet and plumed hats and were mounted on identical gray Arabian geldings.

"Drinking your courage these days, Don Paco?" said Tano Ruiz. He moved up next to Pacote on his right as junior "sword," and his cuadrilla fell into place behind him. "Drinking your eggs?"

Mother of God, was he that obviously tight?

There was nothing to answer. Pacote twisted his head away to look up at the big clock set up above the boxes, and as he did there was the heralding of a bugle.

The two alguaciles immediately started out into the ring in a controlled canter, the Arabians with necks arched in a bow, curvetting sideways, fussing with their bits. They stopped in front of the presidente of the program while the senior constable theoretically caught in his hat a symbolic key to the gate that would release the bulls. They backed their horses all the way across the ring to head the parade of bullfighters again and people clapped for their performance. Then there was a crash of cymbals, and the band burst out with the first notes of "La Morena de Mi Copla."

"Well, there's the wet-your-pants song," said Tano calmly. "I don't see any reason why we shouldn't start this thing." He looked eager for the fight to begin.

God, thought Pacote, I can remember when I could hardly wait for them to begin. I can remember when I was fifteen swimming across the river at night with Matagatos, our clothes on top of our heads. We could hardly wait to get down to the ranches. If it was moonlight, fine. If not, we'd light a lantern and hope nobody would see us. And then we'd cape the hell out the big novillos with a couple of my father's old capes and never worry much about what would happen if we stumbled on that rough terrain in the middle of a pass with no one around to help. We didn't know enough to be scared then. We didn't worry about the bulls then, only eating. And the time we were coming back that night and bumped into the gypsy girl. She was the first. She was only fourteen, but she was already a woman and muy cachonda, and we took turns with her . . . and . . .

And it was Pepe's voice hoarse and loud.

"Vámonos!" Chaves was saying as he ducked out of their way into the callejón passageway. "Let's go!"

10

PACOTE led off automatically with his left foot, and Tano was in step with him, and the crowd burst into a roar as they strode out into the arena. Photographers were in front of them, backing up and snapping, and some pulling out black papers from in back of the cameras and snapping again. A couple of flash bulbs blinked white in the bright sun, and Pacote let himself dwell on the why of this until he reached mid-ring. Then he swung to the right a bit, Tano parallel to him with his head up and flashing the big smile he reserved for audiences. The two constables headed for the "presidente's" box, the cuadrillas followed, and the No–Do newsreel camera behind the fence swung along with them.

Pacote walked as always, head down, straight-backed, his right arm bowed out from his body, three fingers grasping a bit of cuff. So many novilleros were trying to copy that entrance. He walked a little as though his feet hurt him and there was a slight rocking motion, and yet it was graceful — not the easy, unconscious grace of Tano Ruiz —

but a stiff, regal grace. There was no cockiness there, nor was there feigned modesty, but only habitual confidence and the hard thinking on what was going to come.

"Look at that uncle," said Chaves to Suárez. He had hurried around the ring behind the rust-red fence and was now watching the cuadrillas coming toward him. "Look at him! He walks like a frigging king. I taught him how to walk like that." It was as though he'd never really noticed Pacote's walk before, or was trying to get a last clear impression, so that he would have a sharp image when he consulted his memory in the future.

"Look at him," Chaves said. "Drunk or sober, nobody else ever walked like that." But Suárez was too busy to look, too occupied in unpacking the capes and fitting the short notched dowels into the muletas.

The men were up to the fence now in the shade, and, looking up at the presidente of the program, they made a slight bow. The presidente today was the civil governor, and sitting on either side of him to advise him were Juan Belmonte and El Gallo. Pacote made the brief bow stiffly, his hand on his montera, and then he went to the fence, shedding the dress cape as he did.

Suddenly he remembered. He hadn't clipped Belmonte's medal onto the neck chain; it was sitting back in the hotel in his pants pocket.

"Don Eduardo?" asked Chaves reaching over the fence and taking the little ornate cape.

"I don't care," said Pacote. "Sure. Don Eduardo." It bothered him about the medallion. In his semi-drunkenness, it bothered him greatly.

Chaves went down the passageway till he came to where Eduardo Miura was sitting in the front row. He handed the cape up to him, and Miura smiled broadly and spread it out on the railing in front of him.

The parade was over, the monos were cracking their whips behind the mules as they went through the gate fast, and the picadors were jogging their nags out, when suddenly the band swung into the pasodoble "Pacote."

The entire plaza stood up as though rehearsed. The men took off their hats and everyone was applauding.

"It's for you, chico," said Chaves. "Go out."

"Christ in His pain," Pacote said.

But he took a few uncertain steps away from the fence and doffed his montera. He started to turn back, but the applause swelled and Chaves was waving him out with his hand, saying, "A los medios, a los medios."

He walked out a little further to the edge of the shade and stopped. But the people began to chant, "A los medios!" in unison, so he walked out into the sun to the very center. Unsmiling and swearing under his breath, he pivoted slowly, his head bowed, the sun making the gray streak in his hair look white.

It will be great if I vomit out here now, he thought. He looked over at the sunny side of the ring and saw a large sign painted on cloth hanging down saying "Club Pacote of Madrid."

They'll change the name to Club Tano Ruiz after today, he thought.

As he walked back, many people were singing the words to the pasodoble along with the band:

"Pacote, Pacote, greatest torero . . .
From the region of the caliphs you came to become the
caliph of bullfighting. . . ."

And he was moved and ashamed, ashamed of being tight, ashamed of what he was going to do this afternoon. He could never fight down his guilty sense of obligation to an audience, people who had actually paid money to see him — him, Paco Torres, who had been so poor and frail and had run home to his mother with his first money, five whole pesetas that he had made pitching manure. And now they were applauding *him*, telling him they were grateful for the hundreds of afternoons of *emoción* he had given them with his guts and skill, hoping this last one, too, would exhilarate them and give them something to talk about in the cafés and make them say to their grandchildren, "But you should have seen Pacote, the great Pacote, now there was a *real* uncle!"

As he came back to the fence, the audience and the other toreros and the ring servants were still applauding, and Chaves had his dark glasses off and was dabbing at his eyes with his wig.

Pacote cleared his throat and swallowed. "And what's the matter with you, onion head," he said as he put on the montera.

"I got a piece of manure in my eye," said Chaves.

The music stopped, and Suárez handed Pacote the big folded magenta fighting cape. He dragged it over the fence and swirled it open on the sand, holding an end with one

hand. He flipped it over slowly to the yellow side with his name stenciled on it and then back again to get the feel of it. The way he handled it, it looked like part of him. It looked as though he'd never had one out of his hands.

Tano Ruiz was fifteen feet away swinging his cape in the verónica pass, ending with a flashy serpentina for the crowd.

"Lots of salt," said Suárez, contemptuously. "A real salt shaker, that uncle."

"My aunt Sinforosa looks good without a bull too," said Chaves, clapping on his wig and spitting. "What conceit we have here. That uncle's so conceited I'll bet he cuts his name out of the telephone book and pastes it in his scrap album."

The banderilleros had tried out their capes and retreated behind the fence. Pacote gathered the cape to him, hugging it, and slid into the passageway through the burladero opening that was big enough for a man but too small for a bull.

"Now take him wide and safe," Chaves said coming up next to him, and resting his elbows on the fence. "Solórzano will cut him down for you. Take him plenty wide till Solórzano gets at him with the iron."

"God, I wish I were fighting second." Pacote leaned against the fence weakly, and his face was yellow, like the inside of his cape. Little pearls of sweat stood out on his upper lip. "I don't feel good. I feel rotten."

The ring was empty now, terribly and completely empty, a circle of sparkling golden sand waiting to blot up his blood. The drum rolled and the crowd hushed. The bugle bleated out, cracking on the last note, the rope that went to the latch was jerked, and the toril door swung open.

Nothing happened.

Cascabel, safely behind the fence, swung his cape several times in front of the dark tunnel. Suddenly a greenish-black shape exploded from the darkness and skidded out into the sun. Babilonio, number 55 branded big on his side, was low in the haunches, swelling up to great shoulders and the angry hump of tossing muscle. The dust from the corral blew off the muscled back as it ran fast around the empty ring, feinting with its horns and looking for something to kill. It had not been goaded or irritated or injured in any way — not even by the sting of the identifying "divisa" ribbons which most other plazas jabbed into the bull's shoulders — yet it knew what it was in this arena for. It was a Toro Bravo, a separate breed from the domestic bovine, and its natural instinct, plus centuries of careful breeding behind it, told it that it was here to fight and kill. It hadn't eaten this day, any more than the men who were to fight it had, but its fat barrel and sleek hide showed that all its life it had had plenty of the best food. Though it was fairly small, the audience applauded the bull's conformation, the small hoofs, the uniform horns, the silky tail that almost touched the ground. It could turn faster than a polo pony and beat any race horse in the world for a hundred feet. Here was a good example of the most perfect living instrument for killing that man could devise.

Tano Ruiz moved quickly down the passageway toward Pacote, his cape in his hands.

"I'll take this bull," said Tano tensely. "If you still want to fight second, I'll take it!"

Pacote nodded with no expression.

"I like his style," said Tano.

"Take the bastard then," said Pacote.

Tano motioned to his banderillero nearest the bull, and the man slipped out through a burladero. He came up in back of the bull holding the big cape out in front of him like a shield.

"Huh, huh," the man grunted, "Huh, toro!" The bull whirled and charged. As it did, the banderillero let go of the cape with one hand, jumping back out of the way. Bent over and with no attempt at style he trailed the cape in front of the bull's lowered horns. He was paid only to make his matador look good, not to take any chances himself. Two more charges, the man changing hands each time and giving ground. Tano's old-young eyes were studying every move and hook of the bull. A bull generally favors one horn, and Tano wanted to find out quickly which horn it feinted with and which it killed with.

"Enough!" he yelled. The banderillero dropped his cape and vaulted the fence. Tano went into the ring, dancing out sideways like a crab and calling, "Hoooiii, toro, hoooiii!"

The bull was staring over the fence at where the banderillero had left the ring.

"Tápate!" Tano yelled out of the corner of his mouth, not taking his gaze off the bull. "Hide yourself, man!"

The people in the passageway crouched down out of sight.

"Toro, hooii," Tano called again as he danced sideways. When he saw that the bull had focused on him, he stopped dancing. He shook the cape standing profiled to the animal and holding his arms like a boxer, the left way out in front of the right. The bull dropped its head and charged. Tano took a step forward, one knee bent, the other leg straight and swung the cape in front of the bull's nose. The bull went *swoosh,* expelling air as it hurtled by, jumping a bit, the horns two yards from the man's body. The animal wheeled at the end of its charge, the front legs braced and the back legs trotting its body around as though independently operated. It lunged back again, and Tano waited for it a little straighter, letting the horn go by a little closer.

The crowd was silent. They knew the torero was taking the bull at a safe distance to get the first jumps out of it, to let it know that here was its enemy and to make it settle down to a straight, predictable charge.

Now the bull had stopped charging and was staring, a little bewilderedly, at this strange creature that had eluded its horns. In its four-year existence it had only encountered a dismounted man once, and that was when it was less than two years old at the ranch "tienta" where it was tested briefly for bravery.

Tano stepped back away from the bull and changed his

grip on the cape. Then he stalked the bull from a slightly different angle, standing straight, his back arched, the cape partly in front of his body. "Hooi, toro," he chanted as he advanced, "Hooiii, hooi." He shook the cape to focus the bull's attention on it and not on his body.

The bull measured, wagged its horns, and lowering its

head, charged hard. Tano offered it the heavy cloth, dropping his right hand, which was out ahead of the left, down as the horns almost hit the cape, and then moving both hands along together to guide the bull's course. He didn't slide his feet back out of the path of the charge, so the left horn went by a yard from his knees.

A few scattered "Olés" came from the crowd, but they were waiting for more than this: Sevilla prided itself on being what the gypsies called "Servalavari, the Cradle of Bullfighting," and the toughest audience in the world. Tano crowded the bull from behind after its stern went by, running after it, calling harshly, "Hooi, hooi, hooi!" and incited it for a quick return charge. "Hooi, hooi, hooi," he called as he shook the cape invitingly. This time he held his hands closer to his body and brought the horn by his knees two feet away. The next charge was a foot and a half away and brought a solid shout of "Olé" from the easier-to-please cheap section of the ring. He finished off the series of verónicas with an attempt at a whirling serpentina, but as the cape swirled over the bull's head, it tangled on a horn and didn't blossom out around his waist the way it should have.

"What a shame," Chaves grunted. "And he did it so pretty without a bull."

The animal had charged many times without hitting anything solid. It was winded, and in following the cape in the serpentina pass it had wrenched itself around in less than its own length, so it was glad to stop for a breather. Tano turned his back on the bull, knowing it wouldn't charge now, and also knowing that if it suddenly did, one of his banderilleros watching tensely behind the burladeros would fling a cape in its face to lure it away. There was scattered applause as he strode toward the fence, but not enough to warrant the confident smile he wore.

The trumpet had blown during the last pass, and the

two picadors were already trotting into the arena. They sat solid and round-shouldered on their nags, the broad beaver hats with the chin straps cocked on their heads, lances in their right hands in tilting position. The ring servants maneuvered the jogging horses along the fence, tugging them roughly by the rope reins. When fifty feet from the bull, the monos yanked and switched the first horse around so that its blindfolded and mattressed side and the picador's right leg, encased in armor under his leather pants, were all toward the Miura.

Tano went back to the bull again, inciting it to charge. When it did, he ran backward easily and gracefully, zig-zagging toward the horse in a series of short charges, first on one side and then on the other, never losing control of the animal, and finally snatching the cape away from it leaving it stopped and set up in exactly the position he wanted in front of the horse.

Normally this peón functional process would not even rate the attention of the crowd, but Tano had done it so smoothly — so completely as though he and the bull had rehearsed it — that the entire audience burst into applause. Tano doffed his montera in acknowledgment. This was what he excelled at and he knew it; any maneuver in the ring that involved movement, which depended on his athletic legs. The classic verónica with the feet nailed that depended solely on the wrists to control the bull was not for him.

The bull, fifteen feet from the picador, eyed this new antagonist alertly, head high, wondering if it was worthy of a charge. The monos switched the horse forward a step, and that did it. The horned head dropped as the bull lunged forward and socked against the mattress shield that protected the horse. The picador shot the lance just behind the hump of muscle where it belonged, and leaned his weight over on the pole. The bull kept pushing and hooking against the mattress, its back legs driving, and the quivering but unharmed horse was slammed up against the barrera fence. It was time for the "quite" — the taking-away act.

Tano ran by the bull flopping his cape over its head as he did. The bull pulled away from the horse and the annoying pain of the vara and veered after the man. Tano took him away with a wide, running pass. Then he got his hands right, planted his feet, and waited for the return charge. As the bull came, hard and eager, encouraged by having slammed the horse around, Tano swung the cape as though for a verónica, but halfway through he raised his arms, stiff at the elbows, and flipped the cape over his head and behind his back. "Olé," came from the crowd, more for what they knew they were going to see than that first pass itself. Tano was making his bid for ears early with the flashy butterfly pass.

He held out one side of the cape from his body, like a woman holding out her skirt in a waltz, and he offered it to the bull as it swung around for its return charge. His body was exposed now, and he shook the cape so that the motion would make the animal hook for the cloth instead of his legs. As the bull charged by, he stepped back, and quickly held out the cape on the other side of his body. Stepping backward continually and crisscrossing the bull in front of his body by offering the bull alternate halves of the cape, he led the animal twenty feet across the ring, then snatched the cape away and retreated, leaving the bull set up in front of the second picador.

The crowd cheered, and Tano took off his montera and basked in the applause.

"He's got legs," was Chaves's begrudging compliment. "Plenty of legs."

"Listen, Pepe," said Pacote hoarsely, "I'm going to skip my 'quite.' Can't make it."

"All right, chico," said Chaves unhappily. "They'll howl, but to hell with them." He motioned to Matagatos. "Take this one!"

Matagatos nodded and slipped through the fence. The crowd saw him and there were protesting cries of "Matador!" and "Pacote!" The "quite" was often the most exciting part of the fight, for then the matadors were supposed to take turns luring the bull away from the horse and compete with each other in the skill and daring of the pass; it was when the competition was hottest, most comparative, and most immediate. They hadn't paid such high prices to watch a middle-aged man earn his daily wages doing a routine job. They booed.

The bull was at the horse now, and Matagatos came up behind it methodically, chanting: "Toro, toro." The horned tribe held little terror for Matagatos, for he had great experience, and he also knew no one expected anything of a banderillero. He could look clumsy and cowardly and even throw down his cape and pile over the fence if he found himself in a tough spot, and no one would care. There was no hot competitive spirit or ambition driving him; his only function in the ring was to help the big boy look good and try to protect him if he got in trouble.

The bull swung away from the horse and went at the magenta sail which Matagatos contrived to make the first thing to attract its attention. Instead of holding his ground standing straight and guiding the bull by, the way a matador would have been required to do, Matagatos crouched over safely, knees bent, his feet ready to dance out of danger, his arms holding the cape out as far from his body as possible. In a series of unaesthetic, jittery, choppy passes, he maneuvered the bull away from the horse, into position in front of the first picador. The public booed Matagatos as he slid back through the fence, and he smiled up at them cynically. They were really booing Pacote's failure to appear.

"A sweet bull," Chaves observed, as he watched the bull charge willingly back to more punishment from the picador's lance. "I wish you'd been able to take it. It's sweeter than the sea. I knew it would be sweet when I saw it in the corral."

Pacote was holding the cool clay jug up with both hands and letting a thin stream of water spurt into his mouth. He washed it around in his mouth and then spat it out. He turned and glanced up at the crowd in back of him. There was the old Duchess of Peñaranda right back of him up in the first row, looking young with her deep tan and white teeth. With her was Timo, her son, the young duke, looking very British in spite of his Andaluz hat. And then he ran his eyes up over the cushion salesman with four cushions balanced on his head, and beyond the Prussian-looking General Queipo de Llano, and beyond Sweetie Seras and the Aero Club group, and beyond the men bawling "Gaseosa — soda pop, sherry, crab claws," — and there was Socorro.

11

SHE WAS SITTING with a well-dressed, fat, dark-skinned man, and they were not watching the ring. The man was turned to her, resting his forehead in the fingers of one hand, and she was wearing that expression of complete absorbtion that a woman gets only when the other person is talking about her. They seemed to be alone; he couldn't spot any of "the group" on either side of them. It irritated him that he felt something big inside of him when he looked at her.

He made himself move his eyes on, and he saw several people he knew down from Madrid. He saw the old degenerate Raimundo Negro who never buttoned his collar and wore a dirty white coat and hadn't much money but managed to get to almost every fight Pacote had ever fought in Spain. And there was the Mexican, Arruza, with his young, attractive mother. He'd be fighting today in some plaza if he hadn't cut his hand. And near him the torera, Conchita Cintrón, big-jawed but pretty, sitting with the people who'd come over from Lisbon. And there were the Sotomayors down from Córdoba. Pacote had worked on their ranch as a plasterer's assistant, and it was they who had given him his first chance to get in the practice ring with fighting calves. And there were the Aznars down from Bilbao, and Tana, the Duque de Alba's daughter.

Ordinarily he'd be glad that friends had come all the way across Spain to see him fight, but today he wished that everyone had stayed home, or that only strangers were going to see what he was going to do. In back of the Aznars was Felix Cameno, the slick gentleman torero down from Barcelona sitting with a good-looking girl in a white mantilla, explaining what was going on in the ring and mentally planning his own campaign for that evening. And there was fat Salazar of the A.B.C., who was already scribbling in his notebook: "Tremendous heartfelt ovation from jammed Maestranza plaza, taken in los medios, great Pacote, fighting Sevilla for first time in two years, ceded to younger rival first bull, fine Miureño of caste and nerve but presenting no problems to the Madrileño. This one, after series of disappointing, vulgar verónicas, went on to show he admits few superiors in act of 'quite.' Mariposa, pass one seldom sees done well nowadays and . . ."

Pacote spotted the American couple across the aisle from Salazar. She was wearing a black mantilla and it didn't look right on her. He was wearing a broad-brimmed Sevillano hat and it didn't look right on him either. The person who sold him the hat should have told him you have to take off your tie to be castizo. Suddenly Pacote saw them leap up shouting, and so did the rest of the people, and he snapped his head back to the ring.

Tano had taken the bull away from the horse for his

final "quite" and he was down on his knees, the cape
flashing over his head, the bull's horn slicing by his shoulder only a foot and a half away. "Olé," came from the
crowd. The next pass was even closer and "Olé!" came
from the crowd again, and still Tano was on his knees
urging the bull to charge again and when it came this
time and the horn went by the man's body less than a foot
away, a great "OLE!" burst from the crowd as though from
a single throat. Tano hopped to his feet and stalked disdainfully away from the bull, raking the applauding crowd
with his eyes, his jaw out aggressively, and then, as though
his belligerence were melted by the applause, he smiled his
best little-boy smile at them.

"God, wasn't that wonderful," said Helen Newton, applauding after other people had stopped. "What do you
call that one?"

"I don't know," said her husband, "but wait till Pacote
gets out there."

"I wonder why he didn't go out for his what-you-m'call-
it, his turn."

"He's just waiting to wow them on his own bull. And
God, he'd better be good after this build-up!"

The trumpet had blown for the banderillas, and the
picadors were being led out of the ring fast. The people
began to clamor for Tano to put in his own banderillas;
he knew that art better than any other matador in the
world, except Arruza. But he was wiping his face with a
towel down in the passageway, ignoring the petition, and
one of his banderilleros took a pair of the barbed sticks
with the gay paper wrappings and ran across the ring
opposite the bull.

"See your pal Pacote down there in the passageway," said Newton to his wife. "He looks calm as hell. I guess he just doesn't know the meaning of fear."

"He looks so damned aristocratic, doesn't he?"

"He looks so damned Spanish. I've got to get an awful lot across in this article. I've got to show how completely Spanish he is, and how this — this idolatry of him stems from Spain's national inferiority complex."

The man in the seat in front of the Newtons was squirting a red jet into his mouth from a small brown wineskin with "Pamplona" stenciled on it. He turned and offered it to the American. Newton smiled and shook his head, taking a silver flask partly out of his pocket in answer. The man smiled back understandingly and turned around.

Tano's man was running toward the bull, but at an angle, quartering the circle. The bull was charging fast but the man had the angle and the orbit gauged right, and he sidled past the horns, planted the sticks, and scuttled away while the animal's momentum carried it in the other direction. There was only desultory applause; the sticks could be a separate art when it was done by an athlete willing to risk his life, but this way it was just another way of weakening the bull's neck muscles to prepare him for the last act.

"You know," Newton went on, "they don't have all the national heroes we have, I don't know quite why, they just don't, but in spite of all the idolizing, if Pacote were killed today — and I've got to get this across too somehow — if he were killed today, and he died a brave, dramatic Spanish death, in spite of all the yapping and wailing that would go on, in his heart of hearts every Spaniard would be glad that he died. You see, this guy is Spain. They're crazy about death, and to them this guy sort of symbolizes death and yet defies it."

"Oh, Robert, for God's sake, have a drink, and shut up. Look at him down there. He's cool as a cucumber. He's not going to get killed — he's going to stand them on their ears."

The last banderillero had placed his shafts, and the trumpet for the final — and most important — third of the fight was sounded. The bull was wandering along the boards alone, occasionally jerking his neck around to try to get at the annoying banderillas which dangled from his shoulders.

"Now let's see what this new fenómeno has got," said Chaves as Tano, in the arena, was handed the folded muleta and the wooden sword over the fence. Tano took off his montera quickly and neatly so as not to muss his hair.

"The jug," said Pacote. "My mouth's a desert."

"You don't want to get filled up with water."

"I spit most of it out." He drank and watched Tano bow to the presidente of the program and then walk out further into the ring. "I spit nearly all of it out."

As soon as he stepped out of the brown-purple shadow cast by the rim of the plaza, the sun hit him and made him a shaft of green and gold, sparkling in his "suit-of-lights." Holding the folded muleta in his left hand and the sword across it, he extended his right arm offering the montera to the crowd. Leaning back like a tenor reaching for the third balcony, he pivoted slowly, and when he had included the whole audience, he tossed the hat over his shoulder, casually. The crowd applauded the dedication.

"Dando coba," said Chaves automatically. "Sucking up."

Now he swaggered slowly toward the bull, shaking out the red muleta, and as he did a sunny-side humorist falsettoed between cupped hands: "Amado mío . . ."

This was a crack at his too-pretty face and his round woman's behind, because Rita Hayworth sang the song in a movie currently playing in Sevilla. Most of the crowd got it, and there was some laughter. Someone else yelled, "Ay, Rita, so many curves and me without brakes!"

But Tano was too busy concentrating on the bull and fixing the muleta to hear. The red cloth hanging from the doweling rod was half the size of the big magenta cape, and hence twice as dangerous to work with since the bull would be offered less of a target. Tano spread it wider with the sword point, and holding both the sword hilt and the muleta stick in his right hand, he slid his feet over the sand cautiously, his glance going back and forth from the still cloth to the bull standing attentively twenty feet away.

It was a different animal now than the one that had charged gaily into the ring fifteen minutes ago. It was wary, more deadly, defensive. The Miura knew now that it was fighting for its life, that every charge counted if it was going to get this creature who was after it, this confusing green-and-gold-and-red-flowing thing that always seemed to swirl out of the way, or if once reached, became a nothingness horns couldn't get into.

The bullfighter knew he was fighting a deadlier enemy. As he slowly closed the gap between them, Tano saw the bull studying his hips and thighs. Going after the unarmed banderilleros had given it a hint that perhaps the postlike object which glittered was more the dangerous part of this creature than the large soft area which was more active and sometimes separated from the rest.

The bull fixed its eyes hard on Tano's body. Tano "crossed" the bull, taking a sudden step forward, not toward the bull, but across the line where the angle of its body indicated it would charge. At the same time he shook the muleta once convulsively and shouted, "Hooi, toro, hooi!"

The irritating voice and the aggressiveness of the cloth made the bull swing its head slightly to the right away from the body and focus on the threatening folds draped over the wooden blade. Tano "crossed" again, and that, plus two more quick shakes of the cloth, made the bull lunge forward. Tano's left knee bent before the horns arrived at the muleta, and his right leg went back out straight. He remained that way dramatically while he described a big smooth arc with the muleta, which dominated the bull's course. He pricked the animal in the buttock after it went by — the *off* buttock so that the bull would turn around ringward and not fenceward into the man's terrain — and he forced the Miura by and around for another pass just like it, controlling it perfectly.

"That's the best thing he's done so far," Chaves said chewing the end off a cigar. "And how many people here realize it? The kid knows a little something about handling the flannel. He understands the flannel."

Tano was standing up straight now, both hands together as though praying and the muleta stick and the sword handle between them. He shook the cape, and the bull charged.

"Olé!" burst from the audience, even before the pass
was completed, for they saw that the man wasn't going to
step back out of the way, that he had confidence in the
stand he had taken. He merely rocked back slightly on his
heels, lifting the muleta before the horns hit it and letting

the cloth drag down the length of the bull's back as the
animal's charge took it up into the air after its target. Tano
didn't step back and he didn't step forward as the bull
wheeled. He stood as though frozen, not even shaking
the cloth, and the bull charged again.

"OLE!" the crowd thundered. And then two more *olés* as Tano stood there calmly, ten inches away from the driving horns that could spike completely through his thigh if they hit him, forcing the bull to charge by him, seemingly by will power.

"Música!" yelled someone in the sunny section, looking up at the bandstand and brandishing a hand at it. It was echoed on the other side of the ring, but the Sevilla bandmaster was a hard man to get music out of. "Música!"

Now as the bull charged again, Tano spun in toward it as soon as the horn had skimmed by his legs, brushing against the bull's shoulder as he did. When he turned his back on the animal and looked up at the crowd, the applause and the cries of "Música" were so numerous that the bandmaster was forced to raise his baton, and the gay, quick strains of a pasodoble rolled down over the plaza from the musicians' box.

"That bull charges on rails," said Chaves. "Anybody could look good with it." But he didn't take his eyes off Tano for a minute. Now the bullfighter was advancing toward the bull, holding the muleta partially behind his body, catching a bit of the cloth with his left hand. It was the pass Pacote had invented seven years ago, that had become a standard in every bullfighter's repertoire.

"Toro, hooi-toro-bonito," Tano chanted, the cape spread out by the sword and jutting out from his body like the sail of a boat running before the wind. The bull charged, and as the horns hit the cloth, Tano swung it back and up, leaning forward on his toes and arching his back like a diver doing a swan. He casually watched the horns and the black hulk hurtle under his arm, and then he spun slowly around away from the bull and was ready for the next charge. Five more pacotinas, each closer than the other, the "Olés" coming regularly and building louder and louder with each pass, and then Tano strode away from the bull to the fence, slinging the wooden sword to the ground as he did.

"With a bull like that he could make it sit up and moo if he wanted to," said Chaves. "How are you doing, chico?"

Pacote was sagging up against the fence. "I'm all right. I'm doing fine. I'm doing rotten, as a matter of fact. Still feel as though I'm going to throw up."

Tano's sword handler offered him the real sword, and Tano drew it out by its red-wrapped handle, the leather scabbard wilting as the blade abandoned it. The blade was purposely bent near its end so that the thrust would curve a course down toward the aorta, but Tano stuck the point against the fence and pushed his weight against the handle several times to bend it a little more. He jabbed it into the folds of the muleta and went back to the bull.

He gave the bull several chopping, wrenching passes. Then he crouched a few yards from it and studied the animal's feet: they had to be together to open up the small space between the shoulder blades for the sword. One hoof was in front of the other. Tano took two cautious steps to the right, and the bull shifted its weight, bringing its feet together.

"Ya!" breathed the crowd; the most ignorant was aware of the legs-together principle — that and the business of putting water on a muleta to keep it from blowing in the breeze.

Now Tano straightened up and held the sword level with his eye, sighting down it like a rifle. With his left hand he furled the muleta over its doweling stick, flipping the red cloth clockwise so the animal would already start thinking *left* and toward the center of the ring for its charge, not *right* and into the man. He raised the muleta to focus the animal's attention upon it. The bull lifted its head, and then lowered it when the muleta was lowered. Tano cocked his right leg, rose on his toes once, and then lunged at the bull. He went over the right horn, the left hand performing its function of following through so that the lure of the muleta would keep the horn from being jerked up into the man's body as he passed over it. And when the man and the animal were no longer one, the bull's charge carrying it fifteen feet away, the crowd could see that half the sword was protruding from behind the bull's hump. The crowd applauded, because by going in to kill correctly and placing the sword where it should be placed, the man had exposed his life, had invited a pierced lung, as at no other time during this encounter.

"The beast will spit it out," Chaves stated positively and contentedly. "It went in crooked. Our friend's lost the ear."

The bull was charging wildly now, not feeling the pain of the sharp sword in him yet, any more than a soldier feels the pain of a bullet at first, but knowing something was wrong. The banderilleros were in the ring flashing capes in its face, spinning it to dizzy it and make the sword cut something vital inside. But the animal's shoulder action worked the blade out and it fell to the sand. The crowd sagged back and "oh-ed" with disappointment: they wanted a clean, fast death as much as the matador did. Tano grabbed up the sword and angrily waved the banderilleros away from the bull with it. He wiped the blade off by pulling it through a palmful of the muleta, and then he "squared" the bull again determinedly.

"Corto y derecho!" shouted a back-seat matador in the stands. "Short and straight!"

He went in at the bull from a short distance, shoved the sword in the exact spot, and three quarters of the blade disappeared into the bloody shoulders. The bull stood absolutely still, coughed twice, its flanks heaving convulsively. It sagged back casually like a dog stretching, and then it flopped over dead.

Tano spun on his heels dramatically, holding his arms up to the presidente of the ring and dropping his chin on his chest as though saying, There you have it.

The crowd was applauding and cheering, and a great many men had their handkerchiefs out and were waving them back and forth as Tano went to the fence.

"Mucho teatro," said Pacote objectively. "He's got lots of theater."

The people waving handkerchiefs were still at it and they looked up at the presidente's box and yelled: "Ear, ear!"

"If they give an ear for that performance," Chaves said indignantly, "I'll resign from the profession."

The dagger man of the ring ran out to the bull, and

hooking a finger in the sword-hilt ring, he slid the blade out of the still, black mound. Then he took the leather case off of his short dirk and plunged the blade into the bull's head, two fingers behind the ear line. The coup de grace made the bull's reflexes jerk the body stiff, and the puntillero was forced to jump back to keep from being gored by the dead animal.

The mules were in the ring, and the monos were slipping the chain around the base of the horns when a banderillero cut off one of the ears. The monos cracked their whips showily, and the mules started up fast, the limp bull kicking up dust as its left horn knifed a ditch across the arena, its dead legs working in spasms. The crowd applauded the bravery of the bull and the men who had bred it as it went out the big gate into the courtyard to the pulleyed chains where the men in white aprons were waiting to butcher it.

Then they applauded Tano, who was wiping his sweating face with a towel, as his banderilleros handed him the ear. Tano took it and held it up toward the authorities' box with a questioning, supplicating look on his face. The three men stared back hard-faced, and the handkerchief of the presidente wasn't forthcoming.

Tano turned his gaze away, smiling up at the applauding crowd good-sportedly, and then finally he slung the ear at the fence disdainfully. A hat sailed into the arena, and Tano stooped, picked it up, and skimmed it back accurately from a stooping position. A flurry of hats and cigars came down further along the ring, from the sun-and-shade section, and Tano, followed by his banderilleros, jogged to them. He stuck a cigar in his mouth, and the crowd laughed. His men kept the cigars and sailed back the hats. A full wallet splatted to the sand. Tano took out the bills, pantomimed slipping them into his nonexistent pants pocket, and the crowd laughed. He put the money back and tossed it up in the vicinity of its origin, and it was handed from person to person to its laughing owner.

"Sí," said Chaves, "Mucho teatro."

Tano continued his lope around the ring looking up at the crowd that applauded as he went by their section. He tossed back dozens of hats, a white coat, a woman's purse, and kept a bouquet of flowers, after smelling them appreciatively. Then the bugle's grim notes sounded, and he and his men ducked out of the ring through burladeros.

Pacote took a deep breath and breathed it out hard through his nose. "Well, here it is."

Chaves gripped Pacote's arm tightly, "No funny business out there, see? A mile away, see? Especially on this first one till you sober up."

12

THE TORIL DOOR was opened, and almost immediately a black shape appeared in the ring. It stood there alertly, then turned around to see where it had come from, then spun back facing the ring, looking up at the strange, buzzing phenomenon of the crowd, its tail switching nervously. Matagatos, ten yards down the ring from the animal, stepped out of the burladero and waved the cape, holding it in one hand. The bull came at him fast, running low. Matagatos slipped behind the burladero shield nonchalantly, looking up at the crowd as the bull skimmed by faster than a race horse.

The bull galloped around the empty arena, and then Niño de Ronda squeezed through an opening and ran out toward the bull, flaring out his cape. He retreated hastily when the bull wheeled and went for him faster than he expected. It put on a burst of speed and the man flung the cape from him. The bull didn't swerve after the cape but kept coming after Niño de Ronda. His old-man legs were pumping away frantically, and he could tell how close the bull was behind him by the crescendo of yelling from the audience. He smacked into the fence beside the burladero shield and half fell into the opening as the horns hit the boards a second behind his fat behind.

"That fool!" said Pacote.

"You hired him," said Chaves and immediately regretted throwing it in his face.

The crowd was sitting back down now and laughing with relief and the excitement of it. The bull was jabbing at the boards of the shield; it knew this was an inanimate object and not worthy of a charge, but it worked off steam. The animal turned and went back at the cape, smelling it first and then ripping it up angrily. It was all right when its front hoofs were on it; the tough material ripped fine then. But then the bull stepped off and gave it a rip and the cloth flipped up into the air and hung over its head hooked on both horns. The animal couldn't see, and it trotted around the ring blindly shaking its head. It looked ridiculous with the yellow and magenta shreds flopping, and the crowd laughed.

"Great beginning," Chaves growled.

The bull ran hard for the fence, but it heard the echo of its hoofbeats off the boards and slid to a stop in time. It was right next to the barrera. Chaves swore and reached way over and grabbed the shredded capote and jerked it off the horns.

"All right," Pacote called in his deep voice to Cascabel. His tone was weary and exasperated. "Double him for me."

Cascabel, his face very white, slipped out of the burladero. "Toro, h-hooooooo," he called. He had a funny way of calling, and several people around the ring mimicked it. The bull, looking over the fence curiously at Chaves and Pacote, turned around at the challenging voice.

Salazar of the A.B.C. was scribbling in the pad on his knee as the bull charged: "Bonito, number 22, lots of atomic energy, sharp of horn, very gay and mischievous with peones — cost maestro 500 pesetas when it made kitchen rags of capote — almost rang up hospital charges on veteran Niño de Ronda — great expectancy to see the maestro's art as he watched running of bull, planning campaign . . . "

Cascabel took the bull by him wide, holding the cape with only one hand as a peón should and dragging it over the sand just a little ahead of the bull. The bull trailed the end of the tantalizing cape, hooking at it viciously, but following straight and true.

"It's as good as the first," Chaves said elatedly as Cascabel changed hands and doubled the bull back into another charge, giving ground to it constantly. "We're in luck, chico. Sees well with both eyes. Doesn't seem to have an antler preference unless maybe it's the right a little. He doesn't have anything — charges like silk."

In the last doubling, the bull ate up all the ground left to the man, and Cascabel slammed himself through Pacote's burladero with plenty of margin. The audience applauded the good routine job; there was a right and wrong way to do everything in the ring, and this banderillero knew how to run a bull.

"He doesn't have anything," said Cascabel, panting and wiping the inch of sweaty forehead that showed under his montera with his finger. He was as relieved as though it were his bull. "Sweeter than the s-s-sea."

"Run him again," said Pacote, his lips back flat against his teeth.

Cascabel stared at him in amazement. "But he doesn't have anything at all, Paco! No tiene na! Ni na ni na ni na!"

"This uncle knows Latin," said Pacote. "Run him again."

"Cascabel's right, chico!" said Chaves. "No point in running him any more. No difficulties there — like silk, he's like silk when he charges!"

"Now listen, you sons of bitches!" Pacote's voice was quivering. "I pay you two and you take my orders. Run that frigging bull again!"

Chaves shot a significant look at Cascabel. "Run him," he said.

Cascabel shrugged. "Think of all the hundreds of other c-c-civilized professions there are," he muttered as he went through the burladero.

This time he took the cape in both hands; the bull was learning too much about capes and men to get away with the one-handed business now. Cascabel, angry, his jaw stuck out, worked the bull over in a series of fast, rough passes that weren't bad excuses for verónicas, but the crowd protested a banderillero's using two hands for this initial caping.

"Look at that beast," said Pacote. "Look how he chops with that left antler. How did Miura dare to send this treacherous buffalo?"

"He's charging straight as a nun!" said Chaves, alarmed. "If he's cutting with anything it's the right. Can't you see it, chico? Have I ever been wrong? Can't you see it?"

"I see he's an assassin with the left saber, that's what I see. Do you want me to get killed?"

Chaves scrubbed his face with his hand exasperatedly. "Chico, you're — you're blind, you're drunk. But just stay away from both horns and you'll be all right. The bull's on rails."

"I'm not going out with that ox until after the horses."

"All right, all right, chico," said Chaves, trying to make his hoarse voice soothing, "now just calm down and try to collect yourself for your 'quite.' I think you'll have to go out for your 'quite.' Solórzano will have the bull dead by then."

Cascabel was through working over the bull, and he started to run back to the fence, but Chaves motioned him to stay in the ring. The bugle had blown and the horses were jogging in, beefy Solórzano on his black nag first, and El Pimpi ten yards behind. Chaves pointed to Solórzano, and Cascabel got it. When the ring servants had whacked the horse around so that the mattressed side was offered to the bull and the picador was set with his lance, Cascabel began to cape the bull over into the pic-ing position.

The crowd, when they realized they were going to be cheated out of the first verónicas, set up a commotion, and there was stamping and many cries of "Matador! Mata-DORR!" But they quieted down when they saw the bull headed for the horse's side, fast and hard. Solórzano had the lance jabbed in the middle of the bull's back before the horns hit the peto mattress, and he leaned his whole weight on it as the bull banged away at the horse's shield. The bull was brave and kept shoving and driving, the metal stirrup clanging against the horns as the bull hooked the horse back, hurling it against the fence. There, with the horse braced up against the barrera, Solórzano withdrew the bloody pic, already criminally placed, and sank it again in the bull's back, tearing a great bubbling red gash in the flesh. This time the little shield at the end of the pole, designed to keep the steel point from going in more than a couple of inches, disappeared.

The entire audience was on its feet shouting, brandishing fists at the picador and looking up at the presidente, calling upon him to witness this outrage.

"Ya!" said Chaves. "Now."

Pacote shook his head. "Matagatos."

"You have to go out sometime," said Chaves. "You have to go out!"

"I'll take the third 'quite.'"

"You better just go out and make a token pass anyway."

Pacote whirled on him. "Sure, me go out! It's always me going out, while you sit back on your fat ass — your fat ass that got fat by my spilling my blood! Sure, why don't I go out and make my 'quite' while you stay here and count the money you've made off me all these years!"

"Pacote . . ." Pepe's face was white.

"And then when I get a horn in me, what do you care? You just get a new boy, that's all!"

"Paco . . ."

"Well, I'm not going out, see? Matagatos is going out!"

Matagatos caught Pacote's signal and came up behind the bull leisurely, letting it absorb as much punishment as possible. Then when the yelling from the crowd became deafening, he grabbed the bull's tail, gave it a quick yank, and the bull swung around and lurched at the man's cape. The torn meat was pumping out blood, thick, as though a dipper of Burgundy dregs had been sloshed over the black back.

"Crimin-AL!" yelled the crowd, as they saw Matagatos spinning the bull around, the picador getting his lance ready again, and the monos switching the horse out away from the fence. "Asesino! Bandido! Malaje! Maleta! Granuja! Sinvergüenza!"

The brave animal charged again, though with less enthusiasm, and the picador shot the triangular steel point of the vara lance deep into one of the same wounds.

"Son of the great whore!" screamed a man in the crowd, and cushions sailed down at the picador. One hit him in the arm. The bugle blew, but the picador kept grinding the pike into the animal's back. "Assassin, mother-raping butcher!"

Pacote sucked in air through his teeth as he watched, as though the vara were gouging his own back. He admired and respected purebred bulls more than anything in the world. Much more than the finest blooded horse. Pero, qué se hace — but what was one to do?

Even Chaves who had engineered it was wincing at the punishment the animal was taking. But one had to look at it like this: it was a question of the man's life or the bull's.

and the bull would be dead in ten minutes anyway, and then this pain it was feeling now wouldn't exist and would never exist for it again. But the fiesta brava could be bloody ghastly when it wanted to be, as well as bloody beautiful. Who was it that said it was indefensible but irresistible?

"Toro, hooii!"

Tano Ruiz was standing up close to the bull now for his "quite" turn, and when the animal finally pulled away from the horse, it went for the cape. Tano flipped the cloth behind his back and was going to take the bull in the flashy De Frente Por Detrás, but after the bull made its first half-hearted stumbling pass he abandoned the idea. Shrugging exaggeratedly to the crowd, his hand out in a "nothing-to-be-done" gesture, he left the ring.

People were still yelling when a sign was held up in the authorities' box. "MULTA — 300 Pesetas," it said, and the crowd cheered.

The horses were going out the big gate, the presidente having waived the third vara because of the bull's condition, and Solórzano was protecting his head with his arms as he went into the tunnel fast, swearing under a hail of abuse and bottles and cushions.

The critic Salazar was writing: "Cavalry justly fined 300 pesetas for rank abuses of the iron, monetary exchange no help for leakage of victim — justification for imposing a fine on the matador for failure to greet enemy or make appearance during first third, but sentiment will undoubtedly excuse him . . ."

Cascabel placed a pair of banderillas, hooking them in

the sedentary bull flat and from the side, and almost immediately Matagatos cut in with another pair. No point in going through a lot of filigree stuff with a bull as finished as this one now was.

"The bull's had enough," Chaves said. "Enough sticks. We don't want them to suddenly decide to hand us that giant substitute because this one's been punished too much."

"You trying to fight my bull for me?" Pacote said, but he doffed his montera and held it up toward the presidente of the ring in supplication. The presidente nodded, and the bugle blew to change the "third" before Niño de Ronda could get in his pair.

Pacote stepped shakily into the ring and slung his unused cape over the fence. The bull was thirty feet away, occupied with the colored sticks that clattered on his neck.

"Paco, listen, get out of there!" Chaves pleaded. "We can say you're sick."

"Water," said Pacote.

"Just go to the infirmary," said Chaves, scratching the back of his hand nervously. "We'll tell them it was an attack."

"Water!" Pacote commanded, and Suárez handed him the red clay jug. He watched the bull out of the corner of his eyes as he shot the cold stream into his mouth. He was just as dry when he put the jug down.

"Get him out of where he is," said Chaves. "He's in his querencia. For God's sake don't take him in there."

Pacote made the sword signal, a slight jabbing motion with index and second finger, and Suárez pushed it over the fence. It was the real sword, for Pacote had never believed in using a wooden one. Too much faking already in modern bullfighting. Fake pigtail, fake passes, fake bulls, fake swords. Let the maricones — the delicate Tano Ruizes — pamper their frigging wrists.

He hooked his fingers in the red ring of the hilt and drew the heavy blade out of the silver-trimmed sheath. He caught Matagatos's attention and pointed his sword down the ring close to the fence. The bull was in his "querencia," that bit of area in the ring that a bull arbitrarily takes as his own, where he fights a defensive, choppy, impossibly dangerous fight. He had to be lured out of that part of the ring to where he would charge long and freely. Pacote held the folded muleta in his left hand and laid the sword across it, clamping the blade down against the muleta stick with his thumb. He took off the montera and held it by one kinky knob. Then when he saw Matagatos had the bull caped down the barrera to where he wanted, he walked along the fence until he was in front of the presidente's box. He held up the montera, his dry lips forming the routine request for permission to kill the animal. The presidente nodded. Pacote tossed the montera over his shoulder, and the sword handler caught it. Pacote held the sword in his right hand and shook out the muleta. He took a deep breath and started toward the bull, walking the slow, solemn, arrogant walk that was his trademark. The crowd hushed expectantly.

And then it happened. When he was ten yards from the animal it happened. Somehow he stepped on the skirt of the muleta, stumbled, and pitched forward.

If he walked like a high priest going up to the holy altar, when he fell it had the same effect as a priest's falling. To see the dignified form sprawl on the sand shocked the crowd, and when they laughed it was not because they thought it was funny but out of embarrassment.

As Pacote slowly started to get up, Chaves suddenly yelled from the passageway. "Look out! *Cuidado!*"

The bull was charging as Pacote got to his hands and knees. Helplessly he watched it coming at him, saw its head down, the wild little eyes, the clacking banderillas, its summit red with the sheen of fresh blood pumping down over the dried black stains. There was no chance to get to his feet, no time to run if he did manage to stand up, and the muleta was out of reach. He could do nothing but watch it bear down on him.

So I am to die today after all, he thought, and in this ridiculous position too.

"Toro!" Cascabel yelled as he lept forward.

Pacote saw the sudden flash of the banderillero's cape between him and the bull. The animal swerved to hook the more enticing target, but it was too late. Its momentum carried it into Pacote even though it was trying for the cape. The bulk of the bull's shoulder smashed into the man's chest, and he was hurled back to the sand, bloody and unconscious.

The people in the crowd were on their feet as though lifted up by their own great gasp.

"He's dead!" Helen Newton screamed.

Chaves and Matagatos were in the arena gathering up

Pacote's limp body. Cascabel had lured the bull fifteen feet away and was holding its interest in his cape while the men handed Pacote's body over the fence to Niño de Ronda and Suárez. Then Chaves squeezed his bulk back out of the ring, and after putting his hand under Pacote's dangling head, they went down the passageway fast.

13

THE DOCTOR had been watching the fight from a place in the callejón near the infirmary, but the moment he saw the accident he ran up the tunnel. He had to unlock the door — expensive instruments had a way of disappearing — but still he was in his white uniform and ready when the three men panted into the small clinic.

"Easy, easy." Chaves was puffing. "For God's sake take it easy."

Matagatos came in after them. They laid Pacote's thin form on the operating table, and the doctor quickly ripped open the bloody shirt and vest. Chaves didn't look at Pacote — he watched the expression on the doctor's face as he went over the torso, the arms, the legs.

The doctor shook his head. He was young, but he knew a lot about the injuries that occur in a plaza de toros.

"Cornada?" Suárez asked anxiously. "Horn wound?"

"Nothing."

"I knew it," said Chaves with a wheeze of relief. "It was dry. I knew it was dry as dust."

"A lot of blood," said the doctor, "but all cattle blood. We'll try to bring him to now. Hand me that bottle over there."

It was fifteen minutes before Pacote flopped his head to one side and mumbled something unintelligible. It was another five before he was fully conscious and able to sit up on the edge of the table.

"Got to get back there," he said groggily as he tucked in his shirt. "Got to finish that damned animal."

"You don't know how long you've been out," said Chaves. "That ox is butchered and ready for the pot by now. Ruiz had to kill him. I think you ought to let him kill your next one too. Don't you, Doctor?"

"Like hell!" said Pacote, getting off the table.

"I would think so," said the doctor reluctantly. "Yes. You might have some ribs broken or a slight concussion or something there. I haven't given you a thorough examination yet."

"Sure, he's in no condition to go out," said Chaves.

Pacote hesitated. He sat down on the operating table again. It was cool and secure here in the infirmary. Out there it was hot and vicious and full of fear. The pain in his chest and the caress of the infirmary-excuse made him want to sag back and sleep and wake up to find that Tano Ruiz had killed the other bull — the last bull of his life — and then the nightmares would be gone forever. But there was no real hesitation. You couldn't bow out sprawled out on the sand without even a token pass.

"Ya," said Pacote, standing up shakily. "Now."

"All right." Chaves said unhappily, but he knew that protesting would do no good. "Let's go."

"I certainly don't advise it," said the doctor, not vehemently, but as though protecting himself against any possible repercussions; he wanted to see the great Pacote perform as much as anyone else.

Pacote combed his hair and put on the montera, and the raising of his arms hurt. One sleeve was split up to the shoulder, his clothes were rusty with the dried bull's blood, and he was barefoot. It hurt when he breathed. It felt as though all his ribs on the left side had splintered and were sticking into his heart and lungs. It would be good not to have to go back.

"Your slippers are in the passageway," said Suárez.

Pacote walked out the door, and his picadors were there dismounted.

"Nothing," he said to them, and kept going down the tunnel to the sun that blinded him now that his eyes had become used to the infirmary's electric light. He heard the music playing gaily, and when he stepped into the passageway he saw Tano spinning away from the bull after having placed a pair of banderillas, arms high, fingers spread, bouncing away stiff-legged into the roar of the crowd.

Tano ran to the fence, snatched another pair of the barbed sticks from a ring attendant, and went back to the bull. He loped up to it easily, holding both banderillas out in front of him in his right fist as though fending off the horns. He circled around the animal, and when it started after him he put on a casual burst of speed and stayed five feet in front of the horns, zigzagging completely across the ring. The bull could have caught him easily, if it decided to, but Tano stayed just the right distance away, speeding

up and slowing down bewilderingly, so that the tired animal wouldn't be provoked into an all-out charge. The
audience was cheering wildly at his control over the Miura.

The bull stopped, and Tano turned around, running
backward to establish the correct distance. Then he took
a banderilla in each hand and began stalking the bull, measuring carefully, walking toward it slowly, heel-and-toeing
exaggeratedly, his arms coming up from his sides and then
going down in rhythm with his steps. There was suddenly a different mood, no longer gay, but a life-and-death
mood. The bull was four feet from the fence, and Tano
was going to try a difficult maneuver — to place the sticks
while going in between the fence and the bull. If he mis-
calculated by a fraction of a second he would be nailed up
against the boards by the right horn. He stopped ten feet
from the animal and held his arms straight down at his side.
His chin was down on his chest, his back arched. The bull
studied him, shifting its feet, tail switching.

"Toro, hooi!" Tano shouted angrily. "Hooi!"

The bull broke into its charge. At the same time, Tano
sprang forward, but off to the left, headed for the four-
foot gap. He raised his arms high, and as the bull and the
man came together, Tano hooked the barbs in and spun
through the gap, a horn knifing into the boards where he
had just been. A cape, flopped over the fence near the bull
by a banderillero, kept the animal from pursuing Tano,
and he walked calmly across the ring basking in the music
and the frenetic cheering, acknowledging it with a casual
half salute.

Then the audience spotted Pacote back at his place behind the fence, and it applauded his return from the infirmary. The word quickly spread through the crowd: "No injury — a dry blow — it was the bull's blood."

Chaves took off his dark glasses and nudged Pacote. "What's this uncle up to now?"

Tano had the sword and muleta in his hand and was coming down along the barrera toward them. He stopped in front of Pacote, extended his right hand holding the montera, and said: "I dedicate the death of this noble bull to my distinguished colleague who has so deservedly earned the applause of the multitudes for so many years and who now passes with the maximum of glory into the ranks of the immortals of the science of tauromachy."

The crowd applauded.

Chaves belched.

"Horse dung," said Pacote.

Ruiz wheeled and regally tossed the montera over his shoulder. Pacote let it fall into the passageway without catching it.

"This uncle is going to win the popularity prize if he's not careful," Chaves grunted. He moved his foot over and crushed the hat.

Tano started the crowd yelling on his very first pass with the muleta. This bull was larger than his first and not as easy, yet he dominated it completely. He had drawn confidence and inspiration from Pacote's failure. His talent grew bigger than it really was, and he fought better than he ever had in his life before, better than he ever would again. It was as though Pacote, in retiring from the ring, had willed his skill to Tano Ruiz who would inherit the title of Number One. At least that is the way Salazar of the A.B.C. saw it and wrote it.

Tano went through every pass in his extensive repertoire. He took the sword out of the muleta offering the bull only half the target, and gave the animal nine dangerous "natural" passes in a row. He did the spinning windmill pass, the fancy "ki-kiri-kí" of Joselito, and the pacotina. It was as though the bull were completely powerless to deviate from the course the red rag led it. It was so dominated that at one point, after a series of right-handed passes, Tano was able to learn forward and gingerly rest his elbow on the bull's forehead. Then he turned to the crowd, and pointed to himself, his lips forming the words: "Yo, el único — I, the only one who can do these things!"

It was very spectacular, and the crowd went wild over "el teléfono." They were already waving handkerchiefs for the presidente to grant an ear.

"All the tricks," said Chaves. "Next he'll be giving us la televisión."

"He's all right," said Pacote, admiringly, too sick for jealousy. "Everything's easy for him." He discovered by pressing his hand on his left side that his chest didn't hurt so much. But he still felt nauseated and weak.

Hats were sailing into the ring. Tano picked up one and hung it on the right horn. The animal looked ridiculous. He took another and placed it on the bull's head between the horns, making it look like a mule with a straw hat. Most of the crowd cheered, although there were some protests.

"And so noble," said Pacote, grimacing. "What a thing to do to such a noble bull. Kill it, sure, but don't make fun of it."

The bull shook its head, and the hats fell off. Tano went to the fence and traded swords. Then he lined the bull up.

"Both ears if he swords right," Chaves predicted.

Tano went in for the kill well, but the sword struck bone and flew out. The crowd "oh-ed," but Tano quickly gave the bull several more spectacular passes to make them forget the unlucky sword thrust. Then he tossed aside the muleta and picked up a broad-brimmed hat from the ground. Using the hat, and only the hat, to divert the bull's attention from his body, he went in to kill again. He got away with the suicidal stunt, and this time the sword went in cleanly. The bull charged twice and then crumpled.

"Or-e-ja," screamed the crowd in unison, stamping its feet. "Both ears, Señor Presidente! Olé un torero!"

The presidente did nothing. Like an implacable Caesar he sat there, tight-mouthed, narrow-eyed, grim. Make them work for it. The crowd stamped and hollered, and the plaza was a sea of white, waving handkerchiefs. A banderillero cut off the bull's ears before the carcass was dragged out and brought them to the matador. Tano held them up in one hand like two black playing cards, and his eyebrows questioned the authorities' box. The presidente languidly signaled for one ear, and Tano threw one away. The crowd was applauding and motioning for him to take a lap around the ring. Holding up the ear to the cheering crowd, he jogged through the hail of hats with his cuadrilla behind picking them up or catching them and sailing them back. A leather wine bottle plopped down on to the sand, making a rich sound like *thorkkl* when it hit, and Tano unscrewed the top, held it at arm's length, and shot a red stream into his mouth to the delight of the sunny section. But what sent them into spasms was when a crude piratical wooden leg from high in the cheap section sailed through the air and fell in front of the bullfighter. This happened every year — a tribute from the wearer to the matador who was conceded the first ear of the season. Tano laughed and held it off at arm's length as though admiring a beautiful vase. Then he kissed it and handed it over the fence for its journey back up the stands.

Salazar was writing: "Sevilla witnessed forging of a bullfighter today — except for bad luck with foil on first trip in, Tano Ruiz would have . . ."

Pacote looked up in the stands and saw Socorro standing up, cheering with the rest of them. He saw the dark-skinned man at her side was no taller than she was, and that made him smile inside. He saw the American woman throw down a silver flask when Tano passed below where they were sitting, saw Tano pantomime taking a drink from it and toss it back up. A rose appeared on the sand from someplace, and Tano smelled the petals and kept it, tossing the ear up in the direction the flower had come from.

After he had made the round, the audience insisted he take another one. The applause still kept up, and Tano acknowledged it from the fence, but it swelled, and people shouted, "A los medios," and he walked out to the center of the ring. Holding up the rose, he pivoted slowly. Then he clasped his hands over his head and dropped his chin on his chest, as though overcome by gratitude.

The trumpet blew, the ring servants raking the sand hastily withdrew, and Tano loped in to the fence beaming. Except for the "quite" he would have to make with Pacote's bull, he was through for the day, a great day, the greatest of his life. He had cut ears before, but never in the toughest town of them all and not in competition with the Number One. Yes, he'd "given the bath" to the Number One — the ex-Number One, and life was good. He vaulted the fence easily into the passageway, embraced his manager, and then turned to watch the toril door swing open. Pacote still had one bull, and Tano knew in his heart that should the maestro decide to cut loose, Tano's performance might very well be eclipsed. But he glanced over at Pacote's weary, resigned face, and he felt secure.

Number 120, larger than Pacote's first, walked out of the toril cautiously, looking around him. When Niño de

Ronda flopped a cape over the fence it broke into a half-hearted charge. Matagatos went into the ring and doubled the animal several times.

"See, he's cowardly!" said Chaves shaking his head. "I told you at the corral he'd be manso. See how he paws out at the cape with his front legs? He just doesn't want to bury his damned head down in the capote. He'd rather jump on it than hook it. But he charges straight enough. Just don't try anything fancy with him. You'll probably have to end up facefighting him."

The bull suddenly skittered away from Matagatos, and heading back for the safe corrals it had come from, it cleared the high fence cleanly in one bound. The crowd in the stands laughed as two dozen terrified people in the passageway began spilling into the ring. From the shady side the bull couldn't be seen, but his progress could be followed by the policemen and ring servants and photographers and carpenters tumbling frantically over the fence out of the passageway into the arena. It was like a wave breaking, the way one after another the men dove into the ring before the charging bull. Then a gate in the fence was swung open, the callejón was blocked, and the bull trotted back into the arena. He drove at the people in the ring now, and the fence procedure was repeated in reverse to the audience's delight.

Pacote slowly took his cape off the fence. The horses were already in the ring.

"I guess I better get out there," he said hoarsely.

He stepped out from behind the shield into the ring, and

as he did a wave of nausea broke over him, a combination of the chest pain and the liquor and the fear. He put his hand to his head. He felt himself wilt, and he sagged down, fighting it, to the white stirrup board which ran around the bottom of the fence. Sitting there, he vomited.

14

CHAVES jerked Cascabel's cape from his hands, and leaning over the fence he held it around the sitting man. The
crowd was silent and restless with embarrassment.

"You'd better go back to the infirmary, chico," said
Chaves gently. "Come on, get going."

Pacote didn't answer. He covered over with sand where
he'd been sick. "What a great idea this fight was," he muttered as he wiped his mouth with the back of his hand. But
he felt a little better physically, anyway. Better than he
had all afternoon.

He batted down the cape that Chaves was holding
around him and stood up. He picked up his own cape and
walked along the boards. Matagatos had led the bull into
the horse, and now Solórzano was hard at his butchering
trade, his whole weight mounted on the pike. The crowd
was coming down on top of him with screaming insults
and cushions as he shot the lance again and again into the
bull.

Pacote came up behind the animal calling uneagerly:

"Toro ahahahaaa . . ." in his deep voice, the cape ready in front of him. The bull pulled away from the horse and went for the man. The crowd forgot the vomiting and the picador immediately in expectancy. But Pacote bent his knees, crouched over like Matagatos and swung the cape, taking the bull wide, two yards away, his feet jittering backward to safe terrain. He cited the bull for another charge and repeated the safe, ungainly pass. Then he veered the bull into the horse again. The trumpet sounded as the bull charged, but Solórzano kept working, cutting the animal down.

"Sinvergüenza! Shameless One!"

A cushion sailed through the air and struck Pacote on the side of the neck. "It's you who pays him," shouted a voice. "And it's you who gives him the orders! Cowardly murderer!"

Pacote rubbed his neck and squinted up at the sun-and-shade section. That's where the troublemakers were. The elegant shady side was too sophisticated to throw things, and the cheap sunny side was generally too glad to be there at all to get too nasty. But it was those bastards in between who could afford sun-and-shade; they always had to show that they'd been to plenty of corridas before and knew all about what they were seeing. Pacote spotted the shouter who was standing up and shaking his fist down at him. "You call that a pass, you big-nosed coward?" It was the man who had given him the crayfish and the glass of cognac that morning. "You've got your money, why should you bother to put up a decent fight?"

Pacote turned away, hugging his cape to him and holding

his chest where it hurt. Tano Ruiz had taken the bull away from the horse and was doing the flashy spinning lighthouse pass,. and the crowd left off booing the picador to cheer the matador.

"Así se torea!" yelled someone. "That's the way a bull is caped!"

When Tano had finished, Pacote heard the crayfish man and his friend singing to the tune of the pasodoble "Pacote": "Pacote, Pacote, you couldn't even handle a robust rat if confronted by one in the doorway of a latrine."

Matagatos had a pair of banderillas in the bull before the picadors were even out of the ring, and Cascabel was right behind him. Niño de Ronda placed his by sneaking up in back of the bull safely to slide them over flat and from the side, and men in the crowd protested this illegality, half standing in their seats and wagging protesting forefingers down at the action, shouting, "No, señor, así no — not that way here in Sevilla! You're in Sevilla now!"

The bugle blew. Pacote rinsed his mouth out with water and took the sword and folded cloth. He bowed to the presidente and then walked back in front of Chaves. He didn't make a production of it. He said simply: "The last bull of my life goes for José Chaves, without whom I would be nothing." Then he handed him the hat, and they embraced briefly.

He started out to the bull with no attempt at style or build-up. When the animal charged he gave it a wrenching, punishing pass from a safe distance. Then he pursued it, crowding it to make it charge, chopping at it with short passes, wearing it down more than it was so that the great head would sag even lower and make the sword thrust safer. As he worked away on the bull, sweating with the running and the dancing, he held his side with his left hand to press away the pain.

"What's happened to him?" Robert Newton asked his wife. "What the hell kind of an article can I write about a fight like this?"

"It's a rotten bull, that's all," she answered uncomfortably. "Nobody could do anything with a creature like that."

"Like hell. I know that much about this game. It's a good bull. And I know there isn't an article here, I know that much. Unless I write it from Ruiz's standpoint — the clean young aspirant showing up the dissipated old maestro. That might be a good idea. Either that or chuck the whole thing and do a piece on Andaluz folk dances."

The audience was not catcalling or throwing cushions now. They just sat in sullen silence. They weren't angry. It was more a feeling of guilt that oozed into the plaza. They were responsible for the myth. People want heroes, need heroes, but it seemed they had created a hero where there was no hero. It did no good to hear the person in the next seat slap his leg for emphasis and say: "I tell you, I saw him here in this very plaza only two years ago, and I swear nobody in the world *ever* fought like that!"

It did no good, for memory is fickle, and his greatness depended upon the memory of man alone, and when that memory was dead his art died also. He was not a great writer whose books could be reread whenever proof of greatness was demanded, nor a painter or sculptor whose works would live after him. No matter how great people said he once was, the memory of those past times was being extinguished now with every maneuver they were witnessing in the ring. It wasn't because he was too old or because his timing was off. His art was based on a state of mind, and he had not been able — had not wanted — to achieve that state of mind of having to be The Best, of knowing he could dominate any bull that might come out of a toril. Julio Salazar was already writing: "Sevilla saw a pale, spent, stuttering legend of the great Pacote Torres and regarded it with horror."

The only person in the plaza who was pleased with the performance was Chaves. "That's it, chico!" he was calling to him jubilantly. "Echale la mano abajo — keep that hand down — give it to him from point to point — face fight him — tear him down — that's it!"

Someone in the crowd yelled in a bored voice: "Water," and the cry was echoed apathetically around the ring. A slight breeze was disturbing the muleta, and a strong enough gust might blow the cloth across the man's legs and lure the horns into him by mistake. Pacote left the bull to come to the fence, his eyes down avoiding the crowd.

"The heavy one," he said wearily, tossing his muleta over the fence.

Suárez had the yellow-lined muleta out already. He sprinkled water on the edge of it and began scuffing it on the ground so that it would pick up sand and be heavier yet.

"Look!" cried Chaves suddenly, reaching over the fence and grabbing Pacote's arm.

Pacote whirled around. An eighteen-year-old boy in ragged dungarees and shirt sleeves had leapt down from the sunny-side stands, over the barrera, and now was racing across the arena toward the bull. In his right hand he had a patched muleta spread by a wooden stick.

"Little fool!" Pacote muttered, forgetting that this was the way he had made his own bid to be a professional. He put his fists on his hips and jerked his head angrily at Cascabel and Niño de Ronda and Matagatos to be ready. One couldn't try to get the boy out now without risking getting him killed, for he had already slid to a stop ten feet in front of the bull.

"Toro, huhuh, huhuh!" the pale-faced boy was calling professionally as he edged toward the animal. His arms jutted out stiffly, his body straight, his white sandals shuffling over the sand. The Miura waited until the boy was four feet away; it was letting him come way in where it could get a good short chop at him, for the animal was spent and crippled and didn't want to waste a charge on anything but a sure thing.

"Toro!"

It charged. The boy held his ground, swung the cloth, sucked in his stomach, and the bull missed him.

"Olé!" burst from the delighted crowd. This last bull of the afternoon might provide some entertainment after all, in spite of Pacote.

The boy cited again, and again the bull grazed by his legs.

"Olé!" shouted the crowd, and the boy said it with them unconsciously, encouraging himself. The color was coming back into his face, as the first fear left him.

Pacote's banderilleros were hovering around the action, waiting for a chance to take the boy away.

"Move in," Pacote called to them. "Get that mamarracho out of there!"

And the crayfish man was bawling: "Leave him, so that the maestro may learn what close work means! Olé el espontáneo, olé talento!"

El espontáneo, the spontaneous one, was forcing the bull by with close, graceful pacotina passes that were almost as good as the ones Tano Ruiz had done. Obviously this boy was no neophyte — he was an experienced amateur seeking his big chance, knowing he'd probably get fifteen days in jail for it but hoping a manager willing to promote him would spot him, bail him out, and make it worth while. Every pass he got away with was making Pacote's performance look that much worse.

"Get him!" Pacote yelled desperately.

The espontáneo ended the series of passes with a right-handed across-the-chest pass, and beaming at the cheering crowd, he withdrew from the bull a few feet to change his grip on the cloth. Niño de Ronda saw his chance and ran forward. He grabbed the protesting boy by the arm and swung him around back toward the fence.

The bull, incited by the action, charged. Niño de Ronda, with his cape folded in one hand, was helpless. The boy stumbled forward to safety, but the older man was caught up on the horns with a high, woman's scream. He seemed

to hang there hunched up on the Miura's head for an eternity, still clutching his cape. Then the bull lowered its head and snapped it up with tremendous force. Niño de Ronda sailed fifteen feet through the air toward the fence, his hat flying off, the cape streaming out behind him like a rocket's tail. He crumpled on the sand two yards away from Pacote.

Pacote saw the bull pounding forward, the man lying there with eyes crossed and bulging with terror, his bald head stark and obscene above the tanned face, the make-shift ribbon that held the pigtail slipped down over one eye like a buccaneer's patch. There was no banderillero near enough to flare a cape out to distract the Miura. There was only Pacote with no cape in his hands and no time to grab one. He did it automatically without think-ing.

"Eeee-yah, TORO!" came the yell from the deep bellows of the man, and the crowd saw Pacote lunge forward. He reached Niño de Ronda when the horns were three feet from the fallen man. Shooting in between the bull and the banderillero, Pacote slapped his right hand across the bull's nose, just below the eyes. He swerved hard to the side and sprinted for the fence, the bull right behind him and gain-ing, the crowd screaming louder and louder as it gained. But then the man crashed into the fence by the burladero, and Chaves hauled him through the opening to safety just as the horns hit the boards. When the bull wheeled and started to go back to Niño de Ronda, he was confronted by Cascabel and a large cape. Matagatos picked the bab-bling man from the sand and helped him limp to the fence, the blood pumping down his thigh into his faded pink stockings. The policemen had the espontáneo in tow and were hustling him down the passageway.

And Pacote heard it as he helped Niño de Ronda into the callejón. He heard it and found it sweeter than anything he'd ever listened to. It kept up and swelled, and Chaves pushed him out into the arena to acknowledge it. It grew louder as he stood there looking up at them in wonderment, his hand half raised, and God, how sweet it was after the silence and the hate. The crowd was quick to boo and quick to despise, but it was quick to applaud also. It was a good audience, a great audience! Sevilla, the best audience in the world! But there were no handkerchiefs and the applause was not long enough or loud enough. Some people were not applauding — he could see Salazar was not applauding, and the Americans had stopped, and Socorro — he couldn't quite see Socorro because someone was standing up to stretch. And then all the applause was gone, and he took the sword and muleta and started back to the bull. By Christ, he knew how to get them applauding again! He knew better than anyone in the world how to start people applauding!

Now we will see, Señor Tano Ruiz, he thought. Now we will see, all you yelling sons of bitches. We will examine this thing of fighting a bull.

He strode out toward the bull arrogantly, angrily, so straight it was as though he were leaning backward, his left arm bowed way out from his body, his right holding the muleta like a swordsman's shield.

"Toro, ahaaa!" he called, and the authority of his voice and the different way he was carrying himself made the audience hush. It made them stop in the middle of lighting a cigar or taking a drink to lean forward expectantly.

"Now!" Salazar breathed, tapping his pencil against his teeth nervously.

"Now!" said the little man of the crayfish. "Now it comes!"

"Oh, God," Helen Newton said, wrenching her handkerchief. "Now he's going to do it!"

Pacote stood out there like a statue. He was going to wait it out, going to let the horn go by his legs only inches away, the way only he in all the world could do it.

"Toro, ahaaaaaa!"

The bull's head went down.

"Toro, take it!" He shook the muleta.

The animal lunged forward, but it slid to a stop halfway through the pass and jerked its head. Pacote had to jump back and give ground or he would have been gored.

"Ay, caray!" Salazar slapped his forehead. "The thing has ended!"

There was nothing to be done. The animal was through. The picadors had finished it, and the espontáneo had milked out the last few complete passes it had left in it. The bull didn't have the strength or the will now to charge through, to charge hard and fast, charge to kill. Any pass he tried to do with his half-dead animal would look ridiculous. Damn Solórzano for doing it, and damn Chaves for arranging it! And damn himself for letting it be done!

The audience groaned, and some began to leave the plaza in boredom.

There was nothing more to do. After two point-to-point functional passes, Pacote lined the bull up, maneuvering it to get its feet squared away. He couldn't even kill it right, the dangerous, proper way, because he knew it would stay where it was and chop and not charge through so that he could go over the right horn.

"In the lungs!" Chaves was shouting to him.

Pacote sighted down the blade. He rose briefly on his toes, and then ran at the bull, but off to the side, jabbing the sword safely into the lungs, a foot from where it was supposed to go. The effect was immediate and unpleasant. The animal hemorrhaged from the nose and mouth, lurching and reeling backward, tipping drunkenly to the side on two legs, then wobbling to the fence and dying sick against the boards.

And there it was. The fight was over, the last fight of his life, and he'd made it — made it alive. But there was no consolation there, for he looked up at the stands, and the people were putting on their coats and shaking their heads disgustedly and starting to file out the portals, too apathetic to bother to boo the criminal sword thrust or insult the beaten shell of the matador. They were pouring out to homes and cafés where they would tell others, where they would tell the world: "Tano Ruiz, one ear, should have had two, greatest fighter in Spain, really gave the bath to Pacote, always did say the big-nosed one had more propaganda than Stalin and less guts than the Italians at Guadalajara!"

Chaves had clambered over the fence into the arena. He was embracing him and clapping him on the back with both hands. "Aí, caray, Pacorro de mi arma! We made it, you did it, what a party we're going to have! We'll call your mother and . . ."

But Pacote pulled away. He was staring over the fence at the No-Do cameraman and his assistant hurriedly taking the film out of the big double-humped camera and clattering the reel into a tin container. Three days from now that film would be showing with every newsreel in every movie theater in Spain.

A ring servant shoved Pacote aside so the drag mules could be driven up to the bull. He walked dazedly to the fence, looking up at the crowd that was slowly shuffling along the narrow aisles and jamming up at the exits. Salazar was still in his seat, gathering up his notes, notes that would be written into an article that would be cabled to Mexico and Lima and Bogota where he was an idol. Pacote saw Sotomayor leaving, Sotomayor who had given him his first chance to fight. He saw Socorro sitting there waiting for the crowd to thin, making up her face and talking animatedly with her escort. He saw the American writing in a little notebook as he and his wife inched up the crowded aisle. He saw the crayfish man talking with his friend and gesticulating angrily.

And it swept over him, starting with a burning prickling in his back and engulfing him like a wave: *I'm going to do it, I've got to do it, I've got to do it to exist!*

He whirled around.

"Get it for me!" he ordered.

"Get what?" asked Chaves, frightened at the look in the man's eyes. "Get what, Paco?"

"The sobrero," he hissed. "The substitute!"

15

CHAVES'S LIPS echoed the words, but no sound came out.

"Get it!" said Pacote. "Hurry, tell them I'll pay for it, pay double for it!"

"No!" Chaves shook his head and his fat jowls quivered. "No, Paco, I won't! Don't be crazy, don't be a crazy fool!"

Pacote caught him up short by his coat lapels and snarled: "Get it!"

"Like hell — I'm not going through that again for you or . . ."

Pacote drew his right arm across his chest and lashed out at Chaves, the back of his hand smacking hard against the man's fleshy cheek. The blow knocked off Chaves's wig, and his dark glasses dangled from one ear.

Chaves stared bewilderedly at Pacote, wheezing, fingering his cheek, his eyes beginning to water. "All right, chico," he said quietly, reaching down for his wig. "I guess this is the way it had to be."

"Hurry!" commanded Pacote hoarsely. "Hurry, for God's sake!" He prodded Chaves through the burladero and sent him scurrying down the callejón to send word up to the authorities.

Suárez had already packed the canvas cape bag, but Pacote snatched up a folded cape off the top and shook it out.

"Get everything set up, sword handler," he said, picking up the montera and jamming it on his head. "We're staying a while!"

The bugle hadn't blown, and the people were still leaving. He had to do something quickly to stop them from leaving. He started up the passageway toward a burladero. Tano Ruiz was coming down it on his way out of the ring, a cigarette in his mouth, his dress cape slung casually over his shoulder.

"Why the hurry, Maestro?" he said. "The fight's over."

Pacote shoved him out of the way. "Mine's just begun," he flashed over his shoulder as he slid through the fence. "By Christ, it's just begun!"

The bugle blew, and Pacote ran stiff-legged across the empty ring to where the bull would come out. He knelt down thirty feet in front of the toril, swirling the cape out on the sand in front of him and holding the edge of the cloth with his right hand. The amazed crowd saw what was coming — another bull, the substitute bull — and they realized that the man was going to meet it with the beautiful, archaic, dangerous "larga cambiada." There was a scramble to get back to the seats.

The latch was jerked, and the red toril door was swung back.

"Toro!" Pacote called at the dark tunnel, at the un-known, shaking the fist that held the cape. He couldn't see anything yet, but he knew the bull could see him, and he wanted to focus its attention from the first moment. "Toro!"

Suddenly he saw it — a giant black and white shape looming up in the tunnel. Then Pocapena exploded out into the sun.

"Toro, ahaaaaaaaaaa!" Pacote's yell was staccato, like a machine gun, as he called death to him. The bulk skidded around and headed for the kneeling figure. Pacote watched it coming, hurtling toward him, head low, the great tossing hump swollen, and he had to fight to make himself stay there helplessly on his knees with only a magenta cloth to protect himself.

Stay on your knees, you bastard, he swore at himself. *Stay on your knees, you cowardly bastard! For the love of your mother and your dead father stick it out, don't run, don't sway back, stick it out, you ball-less wonder . . . you'll be just what she called you if you don't stick it out . . .*

Twenty feet away, then fifteen, then ten . . .

Now!

Still kneeling, he swung the cape over his left shoulder and revolved his wrist to make the cloth blossom out. The bull swerved at the flash of yellow and scarlet, its left horn cutting by Pacote's head ten inches away.

"Olé!" burst from the crowd as though from a single Brobdingnagian throat.

Pacote got to his feet casually, but his heart was almost choking him. The animal was even larger than he had thought and the horn had come closer than he had meant it to. It was wheeling for a return charge, and he could see the big spread of crooked horns, the whole sagging head lopsided, as though the pinto animal had been made of wax and a flame held under the right side. He held the collar of the cape in his teeth while he hastily arranged his hands right on the cloth. He didn't have to talk to the bull or shake the cape — it was driving back at him now, hard. He waited for it, back arched, chin on his chest, legs straight, feet together, flat, as though screwed into the ground and incapable of being moved backwards even if he wanted to.

On that very first verónica, without knowing how it charged or which horn it hooked with but hoping to God it didn't hook badly, he let the animal's left horn stab by his legs twelve inches away, and he neither moved his feet backward nor attempted to sway out of danger.

"Olé!" came from the crowd, and he didn't really hear it until he thought about it, but then it was a beautiful sound.

He remained motionless after the bull's momentum carried it by, and instead of chasing after the animal for another charge, he stood there like a post, watching the animal hurtle away. He watched the animal hard, watched him gallop on around, watched him as hard as he could, willing him along.

Come on, come on, keep going, torito, keep going on around, beautiful-ugly bull, don't ruin it now, don't make me have to break and chase you, keep coming . . .

Pocapena ran completely round the ring, stopping only to hook its horns once into a burladero and send the slats sailing into the air. When it had completed the circuit, the animal found Pacote waiting for it in exactly the same position, his feet planted in the same spot. It charged hard and from a long way off, but Pacote knew its left side was the good one now, and he waited it out, sweated it out, holding the cape closer to his body, dropping the right hand down as the bull reached him and watching the horn on the lowered head miss his stiffened knees by only five inches.

"Olé!"

On the return charge, Pacote took the bull ten inches away to see how the animal handled its right weapon. Then the bull charged on the good side again, and Pacote worked three inches from the horn.

"Olé!"

On every pass he was showing the Sevillanos what real "temple" was — that rare quality of insouciance and control which slows the bull down to conform to the leisurely swing of the man's arms. Compared to the quick, jerky movements of Tano Ruiz, his motions were a moving-picture film geared down to the last stop.

The bull had a slight tendency to hook to the right, but he took it on that side again, arching in his body so that the horn point was two inches from the gold braid on his legs.

"OLE!"

On the last pass of the series, a tight half-verónica where he swirled the folds up against his hip like a dancer's skirt, he sucked the bull in so close to him that the rounded curve of the horn glanced off his legs and almost knocked him off balance.

"*Olé!*"

A ring servant ran up to Chaves in the passageway. "Niño de Ronda — " he said, measuring off two inches on his index finger to indicate how deep the horn had gone.

"Well, tell them to get him out of there to a hospital or someplace in a hurry," said Chaves, wringing his wig frantically. "There's only one operating table in that infirmary!"

Pacote strode away from the bull, looking up at the roaring mob and hearing the blessed strains of music rolling down to him. The picadors were in the ring already, and he went up to Solórzano, walking along beside the jogging horse as he talked:

"Pic this one right, my friend! Right in its place, right in the cross!"

"But Chaves gave me five thousand pesetas to cut them down!" Solórzano protested, as he set the lance under his arm. "And I have to defend myself against this cathedral."

"I'll give you ten thousand to do it right," said Pacote between clenched teeth. "If you ruin this animal for me, I'll make a steer out of you!"

He told the same thing to El Pimpi and then went back to Pocapena, luring it into position in front of Solórzano's black nag. The bull showed signs of interest, but it didn't charge. The monos beat the horse a step forward, and the bull reacted with a shake of its head. But it didn't charge.

"Talk it up!" Pacote commanded.

"Eee-yah, toro!" Solórzano called. His fat face was the color of sweetbreads and glistened with sweat; he knew that the size of the animal automatically meant a long fall for him. "Eee-yah!" The bull backed up, wagging its horns.

"Work on him!" Pacote ordered, apprehensive now, for a bull that won't charge the picadors is considered cowardly and must be returned to the corrals.

Solórzano waved his lance. He shook his armored leg out of the metal box stirrup and swung it back and forth tantalizingly. The bull pawed the ground, but it wouldn't charge.

"I'll get him charging," Pacote called. He advanced toward the bull and attracted its attention. It charged willingly and hard into the cloth. He spun the animal around twice and then snatched the cape away from its face, leaving it in front of the horse again but at a different angle. It didn't charge.

"Eee-yah!" Solórzano yelled. Bolder with the surety that it would not attack, the picador rode his horse up to the bull, brandishing the lance. The animal bellowed, and Pacote hated the sound, for a bull that bellows generally is afraid. It gave another hollow bellow, lowered its head, and backed up.

"Keep after it!" Pacote shouted. He was panicky inside now. It had to charge, they couldn't take it away from him now! Not after such a great beginning. He was already making absurd promises to God, to the Virgin.

Let it charge the horse, please God make it charge, and I will give up all the money I make in this fight to the Church, I will give up anything, I'll give up the idea of retiring. I'll give up the ranch if You want, I'll give up my life even, if You'll only just make this animal charge the horse!

Solórzano rode right up into the bull's face. But it wouldn't charge.

In all the plaza there was only one person who knew why the animal wouldn't charge and what could be done about it, and his eyes behind the dark glasses squinted with pleasure at his secret and his fat belly quivered with silent joy. He had learned the secret twenty-seven years ago from Joselito, a month before he was killed. He had seen it happen with him, saw the remedy the master of all matadors had prescribed, and never forgot it. Now he saw Pacote spin the bull again with the cape and try once more to make it charge, saw Solórzano ride his horse up to the bull beyond the line a picador may go, and saw the bull, that very brave bull, back up, and Pepe Chaves was glad.

The bugle finally blew, and Pepe whistled with relief.

The gate was opened, and the trained steers lumbered in, the bells that hung from their beige necks clanking lugubriously. They started for the bull, and after a tentative hook at one of them, Pocapena quieted down to join them. They started back out the gate.

"Aí, que bonita es la vida!" Chaves hummed gaily to himself. "How lovely life is! I haven't been to Mass in ten years, but I'm going tomorrow! I'm going every day!"

Then he saw Pacote lurching toward him, tears streaming unashamedly down his cheeks. "Why?" he was gasping. "Why wouldn't he charge? Why couldn't he have charged the horses? He was a great señor toro, an uncle, he wasn't manso! Why, Pepe?"

Chaves put his hand on Pacote's shoulder, his joy disappearing at the sight of the man's face. "Just a rotten bull, chico, a cowardly bull."

"No, Pepe, it wasn't manso, I swear it wasn't!"

"Well," Chaves said, haltingly, "you're alive, chico, and — and that's all that matters."

And in the saying of it, he realized the lie of it. That *wasn't* all that mattered! All that mattered to the man was the fiesta brava, los toros, the being the great Pacote, nothing else mattered, nothing else had ever mattered, and without it the man wouldn't want to exist. He, Pepe Chaves, had no right to keep him from being himself. It wasn't just ego, the momentary sweetness of applause; for Pacote Torres it was survival. And perhaps coupled with that was a fierce, foolish urge to fulfill the people's need for a hero, a Quixotic sense of duty to a tired nation to prove that it could still produce brave men.

"Pacote!" he burst out suddenly. "Stop them!"

Pacote lifted his head, staring uncomprehendingly.

"Stop them!" Chaves shook him by the shoulders roughly. "He isn't manso — it was the horse, chico! It was the horse the bull didn't like!"

Pacote kept staring.

"Maybe from the bravery test — maybe the pic who punished him when he was a calf was riding a black horse! Try him with El Pimpi's horse!"

Pacote turned back to the arena. The herder was still trying to prod the steers out of the gate with Pocapena hemmed in amongst them.

"Hurry!" said Chaves giving him a shove.

Pacote broke into a run crying, "Stop!"

The bull was separated, the steers were driven out, and the gate was slammed. Pacote caped the bull back across the ring into position in front of El Pimpi's white horse. When Pocapena saw the nag, he pawed the ground and snorted, the long tail whipping its flanks.

"Make me wrong," Chaves was praying. "Dear God, make me wrong!"

But the bull was lunging forward now, and it hit the side of the horse with a smack that all the plaza heard. El Pimpi was shooting the pic in where it was supposed to go, where it would weaken the neck muscles but not cripple the animal. The bull's power slammed the horse back against the fence, and then Pocapena stabbed his long horns under the horse's belly. Tossing with the great hump of muscle it lifted up both horse and rider and spilled them over the fence into the passageway.

Pacote was there in front of the bull as it turned away from the barrera, there on his knees.

"Toma, torazo, guapo!" he called. He almost never had done kneeling passes, not considering them true classic bullfighting. But this crowd liked tricks, so tricks they would get. "Charge, pretty monster-bull, charge!"

Pocapena shot forward.

It was the same "lighthouse" pass that Tano had done — the cape and arms going over the man's head, then the kneeing around for a return charge, the cloth writhing and leaping, a beautiful live thing in Pacote's hands. But where Tano had taken the animal a foot or more away, Pacote dealt in inches. The first pass let the horn go ten inches away, the second eight inches, and the third two inches. And on the last pass, he had to sway back slightly, for if he hadn't the horn would have spiked through his head like an ice pick through an eggshell. As it was, one epaulet was hooked off and dangled from his shoulder until he reached up to yank it off contemptuously.

He got to his feet and strode away from the bull into the din of the crowd that reverberated against the sides of the plaza. The stands were already a sea of white, and cries of "Oreja, oreja" echoed around the arena.

The uninjured white horse was led back into the ring, but Solórzano was riding it; El Pimpi was in the infirmary with a broken shoulder. The bull charged hard again, smashed the horse up against the fence, and ripped off the peto shield viciously. Solórzano was pic-ing it correctly, bearing down, but in the right place. Then the bull drove its right horn up into the horse's chest. Like a punctured balloon the animal collapsed down to its knees, dead, propped up against the boards

"Yours!" Pacote called to Tano Ruiz. "It's yours, infant — get him out of there!"

Tano lured the bull away, before it could charge the helpless picador clinging to the fence, and began his "quite." But Pocapena was not like the other smaller bulls — this animal's withers were level with Tano's own shoulders. He didn't have the experience, the nerve, or the skill to handle it. The bull was controlling him, *it* was doing the deciding as to where it was going to charge; the man was just getting out of the way, instead of standing still and controlling the bull, guiding it so that the animal got out of the way of the man. And he made the unfortunate choice of verónicas. The hurried vulgarity of the passes, contrasted with the classic ones Pacote had sculptured, couldn't have shown the crowd the difference between truth and fakery more clearly. Tano ended with a token half-verónica, and then walked into the scornful, deep-freeze silence of the audience.

Pacote held his montera up to the presidente to ask that the "suerte" be changed, that the bull had absorbed enough punishment from the picadors, and the crowd cheered as the bugle blew. The ring servants threw a canvas over the dead horse after taking off the saddle and bridle, and Solórzano rode out of the ring, beaming at the strangeness of the cheers he received.

Matagatos quickly had a pair of banderillas in the bull, and Cascabel followed with another pair, running in to the animal at an angle and then cutting away fast. Matagatos trotted to the fence for the third pair. A ring servant handed him two yellow-frilled ones, but Pacote came up to him as he started back to the bull.

"I'll take a try at the garapullos," he said. "Give me those palitroques!"

"You, Matador?" asked Matagatos. He'd never seen Pacote place banderillas.

"We'll try the lazy man's way." Pacote jerked the sticks out of the man's hand. He licked his thumb and wet the steel points, for luck and to make them slide under the skin easier. Then he broke them over the fence so that the barbed ends were only six inches long instead of thirty inches. He would have to be that much closer to the horn points, when he placed them.

"Las cortas," Matagatos breathed. "The shorts!"

"Ay, Dios mío," Chaves pleaded, "don't get fancy, Paco, please don't get fancy!"

Pacote reached over the fence and pulled the handkerchief out of Chaves's sport coat, wrapping the splintered end of one of the banderillas with it to protect his palm. He took his own handkerchief out of the slit pocket in his jacket and wrapped the other one with it.

"Vamo' a ve'," he said. "Now let us see!"

With his arms at his side, the little banderillas jutting viciously out of his hands, he stalked Pocapena, talking to it softly, friendly.

"Hah, toro, hahaaaaaa . . ."

He walked cautiously toward the bull and stopped fifteen feet away with no one in the ring and nothing to protect him. Feet together, he arched his body and jerked his head back to snap off the montera.

"Pocapena!" he called loudly, giving a little hop into the air. The great head came down and the bull lunged forward.

Pacote didn't move until the animal was six feet away, coming straight at him. Then he put his hands together and suddenly jumped out his right leg, swaying his arms and weight over with it. The bull thought its quarry was breaking off to the right, and it swerved slightly off its course to intercept the flight. But Pacote sucked his right leg back to his left just before the horn reached it, and the bull's momentum kept it from correcting its mistake. At the same time Pacote stretched way over the lethal head to jab the two darts into the hump of muscle as it went by, the great shoulder bumping him back up against the fence.

Pocapena was preoccupied with the banderillas, bucking with the sting of them, and Pacote walked quickly down along the fence to where Suárez and Chaves were. He wasn't hearing the roar of the crowd because he was thinking hard on his muleta campaign already.

"All right, all right," said Chaves gruffly as he wiped Pacote's face with a towel. "Let's cut out this funny business and settle down to some bullfighting. You've sucked up to the gallery enough. Now get to work and correct that hook, and to hell with looking pretty."

"He's charging all right on both sides," said Pacote, panting slightly. He stuffed one of the handkerchiefs into his pocket — he had plans for it.

"Sometimes, maybe," Chaves said quietly, intensely. He handed him the sword and muleta. "But that bull's an assassin. The right hook's still there, and if you don't correct it you're going to pay for it when you have to go over it to kill. Fight him rough and wrenching and let the pretty stuff go by! You'll still get an ear."

"I'm cutting everything today, chico," Pacote said. "Everything."

"Make it brief whatever you do! He's learning fast."

Pacote picked his hat off the sand, nodded to the presidente, and started to dedicate the bull to Chaves again.

"No, no," Chaves protested, "to the crowd — the crowd! They made you, I didn't."

Pacote began the walk to the center of the ring. And then he had an inspired idea.

16

HE WENT to the sun-and-shade section, singled out the crayfish man, and held out his montera to him. The delighted people around him kicked and prodded the unhappy little man to his feet.

"It goes for you and your lungs," Pacote said. "Let us see if we can silence your venom." Wheeling, he tossed the hat over his head back up into the stands.

Pocapena was completely across the ring. Instead of electing to fight in the safety of the protected area along the boards, Pacote walked out to the center of the ring with that slow, measured step, like a king going up the aisle to his coronation. There, in the very middle of the arena, he took out the handkerchief, spread it on the ground, and stood on it. Then he draped the muleta over the sword, and holding it for the Pass of Death, he shook it.

"Toroooooo," rang across the hushed ring.

The bull lifted its head, its snout jutting forward as though smelling the spoor of its enemy.

"Torooooo . . ." Pacote shook the muleta violently.

Pocapena took a step forward and then another, and then it trotted, and then it cantered, and then it burst into a full gallop, charging hard across the yellow expanse toward the tantalizing figure.

When the animal reached him, Pacote raised the cloth slightly. That was the only movement he made as the horns sliced by five inches from his legs.

"OLE!" cracked down from the plaza, so loud and sharp that it sounded like a public address system suddenly flipped on.

He did eight more Passes of Death out there alone, alone in the center of the big ring, each pass closer than the one before, yet controlling the bull so completely that he never had to step off the handkerchief. It looked so easy the way he did it, so safe, as though the bull could charge nowhere but at the cloth. But the crowd knew that the animal went where it did only because the man made it go there, forced it to charge precisely where he wanted by his skillful wrist and knowledge of angles and terrains. Though his graceful movements looked casual and his heavy-lidded eyes remained as expressionless each time the animal hurled itself at him as though his adversary were a hornless calf, everyone in the plaza knew that one miscalculation with this giant animal would result in tragedy. They'd seen how easily it had destroyed a burladero, how neatly it had tossed one horse over the fence, how surgically it had annihilated the other.

Now he held the muleta partly behind his body in the pacotina pass and looked away from the bull toward the stands, toward the place where Salazar and the other critics were. Still looking in the opposite direction from the animal he shook the muleta to make the bull charge.

"Mátame, Pocapena!" he shouted. "Kill me, Pocapena, kill me if you can!"

"No, no!" yelled the crowd, for the man was not even going to look at the animal as it charged, was just going to pray that it charged the cloth target instead of his body. They enjoyed watching a man *almost* killed, but they didn't want to see him commit suicide. "No, man, no! Look at the animal, for God's sake!"

"Toro!" yelled Pacote. "Mátame, toro! Kill me, bull!"

Chaves covered his eyes with his hands. The sword handler began to whimper.

"Toro!" Pacote shook the cape as he yelled. "Toro-toro-toro!"

The bull charged. It scraped by the man but somehow missed him. Five more times Pacote repeated this pass, never once looking at the black-and-white shape before it charged and only catching a glimpse of the stern, caked and green with its own dirt, at the end of each attack.

For a while during the "faena" there had been a kind of music, for each musician spontaneously had unpacked his instrument and made crazy noises over the hubbub, each playing a different wild melody, making it sound like a pack of wounded animals. But now they abandoned their instruments and entered into the screaming.

There were no "olés" now. There was just a continual roaring with cries of "Oh God!" and "Jesús, María and José!" And Salazar, cynical, blasé Julio Salazar, who had seen over nine thousand bulls killed in his life and who prided himself on never displaying any emotion, was on his feet with the rest of them making unintelligible gobblings of delirium. No one could be bothered to wave handkerchiefs — everyone was clutching the person next to him, dizzy with the tremendous emotion that the man and the cloth and the bull were producing. The sun was not on the arena now, and this was not the flashy fighting of Tano Ruiz, as gaudy and gay as a Llopis corrida poster; what was going on now was as stark and tragic as a Goya etching. The newsreel cameramen were recording it all, pass by pass, and it was fortunate they did, for no one who didn't see it would have believed those twenty-four "natural" passes.

He began the historical "tanda" by walking up to Pocapena, light blinking off the sword in his right hand, the
muleta trailing behind him, his body insultingly exposed.
He stopped in front of the animal, offering it his unpro-
tected hip. Then he dragged the cloth up parallel with his
body. He lashed it back and forth on the sand, back and
forth until the bull charged. Without the sword to spread
the cloth the muleta was an insignificant target, and before
every pass Pacote had to convince the animal that the cloth
was its enemy, not the man. He would take it by on its
good left side every time, spinning slowly on his heels with

its charge, and then quickly make him charge again, wrapping the great bulk around his body. Pacote was shouting with the crowd on every pass, caught up by the fever of the noise, sober now, but drunk with the magnificence of what he was doing. Twenty-four passes in a row he did, and twenty-four times he should have been killed. Each time Pocapena came so close that the great shoulder brushed against his body and painted him with blood until the gold of the costume looked orange and the white silk black. And so smoothly linked together were the charges that it seemed like one continual charge, a wind-up toy going around and around the man on its track.

But the toy was wearing down and learning, beginning to wonder if the elusive red cloth actually was its enemy. It was time to kill. The last act of the tragedy was over.

"Kill it!" Chaves was calling.

But when Pacote started to "square up" the bull, the crowd began stamping its feet, yelling, "More, more!"

"More they want!" Suárez exclaimed weakly. "After that they want more!"

"More . . . they'll always want more," said Chaves digging his fingernails into the boards of the fence. "That bull isn't right to be killed yet either — Paco still hasn't corrected that hook!"

"More, more, more!" the crowd was chanting. "Más y más y más!"

"Kill it," Chaves shouted. "Kill it now!"

Pacote looked up at the crowd and shrugged. If they wanted more, they could have more. They could have anything today. He was drunk with excitement, sopped with power, and his fear, his terrible fear was gone. He was the best, the *best*, the *best!*

"Torito!" he called triumphantly, disdainfully. "Little bull! Charge, little bull, charge, little calf!"

He cited the bull for a right-handed pass with the sword spreading the cloth. As the horns reached the muleta, he dropped to his knees and spun around. He stayed on his knees and made the bull charge again. Five times he did that, bloodying his shirt and shoulders as he spun in against the animal. After the last pass, still on his knees, he went toward the bewildered bull. Closer and closer he came, the muleta and sword dragging uselessly on the ground. Closer and closer, and the bull was so dominated by the man that it didn't charge. Closer and closer, relentlessly, past the point of no return. If the animal charged now he would be helpless — at this distance the horns couldn't help but kill. The bull backed up a step and looked as though it might charge. But it didn't. Right up into the animal's face he kneed himself, right between the spread of horns. Leaning forward, he kissed the bull between the eyes, on the kinky hair between its eyes.

Then he took the tip of the bull's left horn between his teeth.

The crowd was frozen, fifteen thousand people stiff with the terrible sight of it. There was none of the small noises, the cough, the rustle, of most silences. There was only deathlike soundlessness as they watched in horrified fascination. The slightest movement or noise might cause the bull to shake its head and send the horn tearing through the man's skull. But, as though hypnotized, cowed by the brute animal courage of this kneeling creature in front of it, the bull didn't move.

Pacote turned slowly on his knees, the horns almost against his back, to stare up at the crowd with glazed, fanatical eyes. Then, for the first time in his life, he smiled in a bull ring. Holding up a forefinger, making fun of Tano Ruiz and himself at the same time, his lips formed the words: "I — the only one who can do these things!"

He got to his feet and strode away from the bull, and the roar of the crowd broke forth. He cast the muleta aside scornfully and picked up his handkerchief from the ground. He lined the bull up until its feet were together and sighted down the blade. He held the handkerchief in his left hand, to use it to protect himself and distract the bull away from his body.

"No!" the crowd was screaming. "No, man, no!"

"Off to the side and into the lungs!" Chaves yelled through cupped hands. "Paco, for God's sake . . ."

But this one, more than any other in his life, had to be finished off right. After rising on his toes and focusing the bull's attention on the handkerchief, Pacote hurled himself straight at the animal. He lunged over the lowered right horn, letting the animal's own momentum impale it on the sword. The bent blade, slicing down toward the aorta, disappeared as easily into the shoulders as though into a mound of black and white lard.

But while the man and the bull hovered in one shape, the great head suddenly jerked up, the crooked horn stabbed hard, and Pacote was lifted high in the air on the bull's head. He could feel the curly hair and see the crazy flopping of the banderillas and hear the wheeze from the wet snout, and he saw the yellow-whitish horn — the pus-colored horn — sticking up into his crotch. He grabbed the base of it with both hands, trying to fight it, trying to wrench it out of his body, but his weight made him spin, head down, and he felt it corkscrew way up into him, tearing through the flesh up into his stomach. And then the horn was pulled out of him with a sucking sound, and he was slammed to the ground.

The bull started to charge again as he lay on the bloodying sand. Suddenly it wobbled, coughed, and fell over dead. Chaves and Suárez were already in the ring, Chaves waddling frantically and with amazing speed, but Cascabel was the first to reach the inert figure. They carried him across the ring, and the gate was swung open for them.

"A little more?" Chaves yelled up at the crowd as he went under the stands. "Would you like a little more, you bastards, would you like a little more?"

El Pimpi was sitting on the operating table with his chest bandaged and his arm in a sling, but he got off fast when he saw them come in the infirmary, and they laid the unconscious man down gently.

"Doctor, it's bad," Chaves babbled, "This one's bad, it's bad!"

The doctor looked at the blood pooling on the table and whistled silently. "Get the clinic right away — tell Quintana to get over here right away! We're operating!"

There was a telephone in the outer room; Suárez ran to it and called.

"You'd better wait out there," said the doctor as he began to slash off the spangled suit with a scapel. "Do you know what type blood you have?"

Chaves shrugged, suddenly helpless, out of character. He shook his head.

They went into the bare outer room and sat silently on the bench. Except Cascabel. He knew what type his blood was, and he was kept in the operating room. In a little while, Doctor Quintana came in. He was in a white uniform, and he went straight into the operating room without speaking to them.

One couldn't smoke in there. Chaves didn't know what to do. He took his wig out of his breast pocket and picked at the hairs, singling one from the others and then snapping it out delicately. Soon his wig had a bald spot on the crown. He carefully examined each square of the fine mesh which was the scalp of the wig. Then he slumped back against the wall and stared at nothing. The others went outside to smoke, but he kept sitting there.

The door opened, and a young priest came in. He looked very scrubbed and good, and he wore thick glasses.

"They said I might be needed here."

Chaves swallowed and pointed to the operating room. The priest went in. He came out in a little while, his good face looking worried. "I'm going for Father Gabriel," he said.

Chaves wanted to ask how Pacote was, but before he could get his nerve up, the priest was gone.

In a few minutes the door opened again, and it was Socorro.

Chaves lifted his face out of his hands. "You," he breathed.

"It's taken me all this time to get through that terrible crowd around the gate," she said. "And then the gateman wouldn't let me through. I had to give him a hundred pesetas. How is he, for God's sake? I saw a priest leaving here. What was he doing here? Is he dying? He's dying isn't he?"

"Dying? You ask me that? *You?*"

"You animal," she said, "tell me!"

Chaves's voice quivered, "He's — he's got a hole in him," he said hoarsely, "a hole they'll never be able to fill."

"Dying . . . oh, Pepe!" She paced up and down. "We love each other — we've always loved each other — he asked me to marry him this morning. And I said I would . . . I said I would after the fight." She moved close to him, her eyes bright. "We can do it now. Before it's too late. We can do it now if we hurry. But we've got to hurry."

Chaves stared at her hard. "I don't believe you."

"I swear it, Pepe, I swear it! By the crucified Christ! He asked me to marry him, but I didn't . . . I couldn't . . . not then, because, well, his nerves . . . you know how his nerves have been . . . but I want to marry him now. He needs me. I'm going to marry him now!"

Chaves didn't say anything, but he kept looking at her, looking through her.

"Well? What are you staring at? Take me in to him."

He scratched the back of his hand. "You love him?"

"Yes, of course," she said. "And he loves me . . . you know that."

Chaves whistled silently to himself. "Then you ought to get married." He repeated it as though trying to convince her. "Yes, I think you should get married."

"Well, that's what I'm trying to tell you! Let me go to him."

"We have to get the priest first," he said, standing up. "He just left — we can catch him if we hurry."

"Let's go, then!"

Chaves opened the door for her, and Socorro stepped outside. As soon as she did, he slammed it behind her and turned the lock. He leaned up against the inside of the door, and putting his fist to his forehead, he shook with silent laughter. By the blessed Macarena, Pacote's millions weren't going to go to any five-peseta whore! He could feel the angry pounding and hear the invective, and it made him shake all the more. But then he saw Cascabel come out of the operating room, rolling down his sleeve, Chaves's laugh melted into a groan and he left the door to go up to him.

"How is he, how is he, man?"

"Gravísimo," said Cascabel. "Very grave. I've seen him hurt plenty of times, but I've never heard him complain like this. You'd better call his mother. Maybe she can fly down from San Sebastián. He's out of the ether now if you want to go in."

"You call her, boy. I can't talk to her now."

Chaves went in. Pacote was under a sheet, his ascetic face gray, the scar that notched the left side of his face stark white. He looked very old and very tired.

"Call your friend, Doctor," he was murmuring, his eyes closed. "Call your friend in Madrid."

"I have, Paco," the doctor said, "and he's on his way." He turned to Chaves. "He means Arroyo, the horn specialist."

"Jesús, what pain!" Pacote exclaimed suddenly, his eyebrows convulsing together. "Can't you put my leg better? It feels doubled up under me."

The doctor looked at Chaves, wrinkling his forehead and shaking his head.

Pacote opened his eyes and saw Chaves. "Hola, the great Pepe," he breathed. "Did the animal die, Pepe?"

"Sí, chiquillo, sí," said Chaves. Tears started down his cheeks from under his dark glasses.

"It died and they didn't give me anything?" Pacote struggled to his elbows. "And they didn't give me anything?"

"They gave you everything," Chaves choked out. "Everything. Ears, tail, and hoof. The first time they've ever given a hoof in the Maestranza."

"That was a fight wasn't it, Pepe?" He asked it like a small boy.

"That was a fight, chico."

Pacote eased back on the table, a flickering smile trying to establish itself in one corner of his mouth. "It's just like God says, eh Pepe? Take what you want — but pay for it." Then he said weakly: "You know, chico, you ought to get hold of that espontáneo. He had plenty of salt, a real salty boy."

"I'm never going to step into a plaza de toros again as long as I live!" Chaves was dabbing at his cheeks with the crumpled wig.

"Don't talk crazy," said Pacote, reaching his hand out feebly and putting it on Chaves's forearm. "You get that kid. He'll have to do some time in jail, but when he gets out of the shade, you grab him." His face contorted. "Ay, ay! What a tobacco that bull handed me! I never had one like this, Pepe."

Cascabel came in. "I called your mother, Pacorro. She's on her way here."

"Gracias, Desperdicios. How she must be suffering." Suddenly he stiffened. "Doctor, I can't feel anything in my right leg."

"You're all right, Paco," said Doctor Quintana. "There's nothing to be worried about."

Pacote lay there breathing hard. Then he said: "Doctor, I can't feel anything in my left leg!"

"That's all right," said the doctor. "You'll be well in no time. You'll be walking around in a month."

"Doctor," said Pacote in a frightened voice. "Are my eyes open? I can't see!"

He half rose up on the table and then fell back.

The doctor examined him. He stayed there with his back to Pepe, and then he reached over and gently closed the dark eyes.

A great sob came from Chaves.

"More and more," said Cascabel dully, the tears spilling down his face. "They kept demanding more and more — and more was his life, so he gave it to them."

"We did everything possible," the doctor apologized. "But the size of the . . ."

"Sure, sure," said Chaves. There were tears in his mouth, and he spat them out on the floor. He backed away from the table and stumbled toward the door. He went out, lurching past the others, not seeing them. It was night now but not very dark yet. He went out into the quiet patio de caballos and through the gate. There was a silent crowd lounging there, and one person asked, "How is he?" But Chaves kept walking, not hearing. He was conscious of the American journalist walking along beside him saying: "Señor Chaves, I wondered if I could . . ."

Chaves shoved him aside and went down a narrow, crooked street, not knowing where he was going, just wanting to get away from the plaza de toros. He rounded a corner and was aware of someone way below him talking to him.

"Por Dios, caballero . . ."

He looked down and saw a truncated man riding on a coaster with children's skates underneath. The man smiled a toothless smile, dropping one of the leather-covered blocks with which he propelled himself and holding out his hat.

"Charity, for God, caballero, charity for the love of God, pity this wretched . . ."

"Holy Mother of Jesus!" Chaves croaked. He groped in his pockets frantically and threw all his coins and the gold money clip with Solórzano's torn bills in it, and a medallion and the keys attached to his lucky monkey's head and his wallet and his cigars and his address book and the comb he carried for Pacote to use in the ring and his wig — all of it he showered down over the half-man. Then blindly he staggered past him down the street.

"Heaven will repay you," the beggar mouthed happily as he gathered up the loot.

THE END